PROF. DAVID PURDIE was born privately and spent most of his early years as a child, before being educated publicly at Ayr Academy and the University of Glasgow. His career took him abroad for over 20 years to England where he was Clinical sub-Dean of Leeds University medical school. He concluded his medical academic life as a Professor Emeritus of the Universities of Hull and York.

He is presently an Hon. Fellow of Edinburgh University's Institute for Advanced Studies in the Humanities (IASH) located on The Meadows, the capital's great public park, upon which he gazes thoughtfully when seeking Enlightenment. Fellows of IASH work in the fields of, inter alia: Philosophy; Classics; European Literature and other disciplines too complex to spell.

David is an Editor of the 4th Edition of the *Burns Encyclopaedia* jointly with Profs Gerry Carruthers and Kirsteen McCue of Glasgow University – and of editions of Sir Walter Scott's *Ivanhoe* and *Heart of Midlothian*. Following his work with Prof. Peter Fosl of the US on Scotland's greatest philosopher, *le bon David*, he regards himself simply as a Humean being.

A Patron of the National Library and National Galleries of Scotland, he occupies a 400 year-old pile with plumbing to match and resident ghost, on Edinburgh's North-West Frontier, i.e. between the New Town and Stockbridge.

The Dean of St Andrew's College is suspected to be a close relative. Any resemblance to persons dead, living, or yet unborn, is accidental.

The Dean's Diaries

Being a True & Factual Account of
the Doings & Dealings of
The Dean & the Dons
of St Andrew's College

PROF. DAVID PURDIE

with illustrations by
BOB DEWAR

Luath Press Limited
EDINBURGH
www.luath.co.uk

First Published 2015

ISBN: 978-1-910745-20-5

The paper used in this book is recyclable. It is made
from low chlorine pulps produced in a low energy,
low emissions manner from renewable forests.

Printed and bound by
CPI Antony Rowe, Chippenham

Typeset in Sabon and MetaPlus by 3btype.com

Contents

Foreword

by the Rt Hon. the Lord Fanshawe FRS

I T IS WITH REAL and unfeigned pleasure that I contribute this Foreword to the long-awaited publication of the *Dean's Diaries* in book form. By far the most formative period of my own academic career were the years spent at St Andrew's College, first as Research Fellow and then as a Don.

Like all *alumni*, I retain an intense interest in the old place and in the extraordinary press reports involving the Dean and his faculty. These include the misadventure of my colleague Prof. Trevelyan in the College laundry chute and the seismic matter/antimatter explosion which blew out almost every window in Edinburgh's Old Town. Of current interest is the Dean's repeated denials of the persistent rumour that the Astrophysics Unit had made contact with an 'entity' within the constellation Andromeda.

Thanks to the advocacy of my learned friend Alex MacEchron QC of the College's Dept. of Scots Law, the Court of Session has finally agreed that the secretive old Constitution be set aside so that the complete *Diaries of the Deans* dating back 450 years may be published, starting with the diaries of the current Dean. We will thus gain insight into the College's role in the development of the aerophone, the self-starting oven and the omnilingual translator. Out of the shadows will come, finally, an account of the creation of the first artificial Black Hole which swallowed the entire Physics Department before vanishing in the direction of the City Chambers.

I hope to be present, *dv*, next September when the College will participate in Open Doors Day. The highlight of this is to be a lecture by Prof. Sir Iain Roberts DD, holder of the David Hume Chair of Advanced Scepticism entitled:

The Virgin Birth; Some Conceptual Difficulties

In summary, the general population of Scotland remains rightly proud of St Andrew's College, seeing in its fierce political incorrectness and general eccentricity a shield against the creeping gloom of the Endarkenment.

Lang may its lum reek in Reekie.

Fanshawe,
President, Emmanuel College, Oxford.

Introduction

FOUNDED IN January 1561 by a Decree of the Regent Earl of Moray and the Rev. John Knox, St Andrew's College occupies a unique position both in Edinburgh and at the apex of British academia. Superintended by its Dean and *Estaitis*, or Council, the College was described recently in a review by *The Times Academic Supplement* as, 'A Titanic of the Intellect'. As a University College it is independent of the City's four other universities (Edinburgh; Heriot Watt; Napier and Queen Margaret).

The College occupies a full city block in King George IV Bridge between the National Library of Scotland and the National Museum at the corner of the Bridge and Chambers St. Intriguingly, it cannot be approached using any GPS device due to a massive augmentation of the Earth's magnetic field by the Supertesla Array used in its anti-gravity work for the Ministry of Defence. This may also explain the recent 'tractoring' into the College atrium of a passing No. 42 Lothian bus, followed by the ATM machine from the Bank across the street. St Andrew's maintains a marine biology 'outstation' at Machrihanish at the Mull of Kintyre. There is also an 'enclave' in the Carrifran Valley in the Moffat hills, the purpose of which is known only to the MOD.

Traditionally highly secretive, St Andrew's is believed to have about 40 permanent academic staff, known as Dons. There are a similar number of postdoctoral

Research Fellows, the Dean recently stating to the BBC that he was 'never quite sure of the *precise* number, as they pop in and out of existence in a quantumly relativistic way.' Many of these come from overseas, including England, their Fellowships lasting as long as their project, or the Dean's patience, lasts. St Andrew's, however, remains resolutely international. It presently houses three Fullybright Scholars from the US, two from the Sorbonnet in Paris and one from the Max Plonck Institute in Stuttgart. College Fellowships rank with those of All Souls College, Oxford and of Harvard as the ultimate 'Glittering Prize', in any academic career.

Regarding subject matter, both Dons and Fellows range across the Humanities with particular emphasis on: Classics; Philosophy; History and Literature, while the Sciences are restricted by space to those disciplines not requiring heavyweight equipment; such as theoretical geology and astrobotany.

Former Fellows include several Nobel laureates including Sir Hector Mackendrick who discovered 'The One' by uniting quantum dynamics with Einsteinian general relativity, and Prof. Aeneas Blair-Drummond who deciphered the Pictish Papers. Current Dons include Prof. Abe Rabinowitz, head of Semitic Studies who finally proved that the Scots are the lost 13th tribe of Judah, and Dr Henry Burns, recipient of the McGonagle Prize for 2013 for his invention of the Bathing Wig™.

St Andrew's has no undergraduate students. Thanks to the Endowment, neither Dons nor Fellows undertake any teaching or administrative duties. They are thus freed to prosecute 'blue sky' research in the manner of such sister institutions as IASH at the nearby University of Edinburgh, and the Institute for Advanced Study at Princeton University in the US.

The College is financially independent, receiving no funding either from HMG at Westminster or from Holyrood. This is due to its massive Endowment, believed to derive from its Constitution written in 1698 in the aftermath of the Darien Scheme. It *deliberately* represented the Scheme as a failure, thus concealing from public view the enormous quantity of gold bullion and silver artefacts brought back to Scotland from the Isthmus of Panama and secreted in the College vaults.

Intense public and press interest in the secretive College and its Dons prompted the Dean to begin releasing his weekly *Academic Diary* in the Martinmas Term of 2012. Revelation of the extraordinary activities at St Andrew's, together with the oddities of the Dean and his senior officers: the Bursar; Warden; the Bedellus and the 'Visitor', constitutes one of the most remarkable documents to emerge from Academia in recent centuries.

'I do this for Posterity, don't you know,' said the Dean in the recent STV documentary *Risen by Gravity*, 'despite Posterity having done absolutely nothing for us... yet.'

College Animals

Office of the Dean

St Andrew' s College
King George IV Bridge
Edinburgh EH1 1EE

T HE MARTINMAS TERM is now well underway – and
the College hums with scholarly endeavour. That
is, when it is not humming with the atrocious pong
coming from our Palaeontology Research Unit where a
complete adult woolly Mammoth is being warmed up

for dissection. Dug out of some Russian ice-bog, it was presented to us as a 'fraternal greeting' by the Sverdlovsk Academy of Sciences.

I really wish we could be spared these very kind but hugely inconvenient 'gifts' from colleagues elsewhere. Last year it was a Giant Squid (*Architeuthis physenteris*) with suckers the size of soup plates from somewhere off the Azores. Its arrival in the Marine Biology Lab coincided with an unusually warm April and had all of us in gasmasks for a fortnight. The thing was so recently dead that when an electric cable touched one of its huge arms it uncoiled, whiplashed across the lab, smashed a window and grabbed Mrs Tunnock the tea-lady, whose shrieks I can still hear.

The animal life of this College is truly remarkable. The sheer range of creatures calling the place home matches the provenance of the Fellows – and their oddities. Yala, the Bursar's dog, is here under false pretences, canines being banned by Statute. However, on hearing how our Oxford colleagues surmounted the problem of the Master's poodle at Balliol, a Council meeting formally declared it, *nem con.*, to be a cat.

This hound is a *Shar-pei*, or rather a 沙皮 in Cantonese, and is the traditional gate-keeper of their ancient religious sites. How a Chinese temple guardian came to be in Edinburgh's dog pound where the Bursar found it, is a mystery to me. Anyway, the creature now guards *him* with assiduous care, fixing all visitors, including me, with an inscrutable oriental stare.

Much more entertaining is *Mnemosyne* our Philosophy Department's Hill Mynah (*Gracula religiosa*) named after the Greek goddess of memory and mother of the nine Muses. Memo, as she's known throughout College, is actually in the Guinness Book of Records for possessing an astonishing 800 word memory. Less believable is the assertion by our metaphysician Prof. Archie MacKendrick that Memo actually *understands* the theory of syllogistic logic and is a disciple of David Hume's approach to the problem of induction.

The bird regularly attends seminars in the Philosophy Department, listening intently to all the positing, conjecturing and refuting they get up to. She enlivens proceedings with an occasional bowel movement and fixes a beady eye on any participant suspected of a logical inexactitude or a dodgy premise. Its suspicion of any such is greeted with a whistle and a piercing cry of '*Bull!*' or 'Up *Wittgenstein!*' thereby reducing the company to hysterics.

However, the absolute star of bird eloquence was the Captain's cockatoo on the frigate HMS *Ganges* back in the age of sail. Orders were then were issued to the jolly Jack Tars by complex whistles on the Bosun's pipe. The bird had learned a dozen or so of these and when the actual Bosun whistled, it would issue accurate but contradictory instructions – to the white fury of the Bosun and delight of the crew. The whistle for 'Admiral's barge approaching', would be followed by '*Abandon ship!*'

The creature also had superb timing. When the pipe was 'Anchor, *hoist*' after a pause to let the sweating Tars get it half-way up with the windlass, the bird would signal '*Let go!*'

Animal intelligence is not confined to cockatoos, killer whales or bottle-snouted dolphins. The chimpanzee, our nearest cousin, is also seriously smart, not surprising, given that it shares no less than 98.5 per cent of its DNA with *Homo sapiens*.

The announcement of this in 2006 coincided with a theological conference here at the College. I mentioned it to our principal guest, the then Archbishop of York who seemed rather taken aback. At lunch, his Chaplain confided to me that His Grace had been seriously unamused to be told that he shared 98.5 per cent of his genetic endowment with a chimp. I said, 'Not amused is he? Just wait till he hears that he shares 48 per cent of it with a banana!' However, by the time of his own Keynote Lecture that afternoon, the Archbishop had come to terms with science. He told a startled audience that since Man's immortal soul is part of the body politic and is thus encoded by our DNA, this means that the Chimpanzee also probably has a soul. Consequently, the care and welfare of the souls of apes residing south of the Border might well become a charge upon the Church of England... My Lord Archbishop did not produce any consensus for this extraordinary conjecture, but he reckoned without the presence of the Press. The result next day was a splendid headline over the *Daily Telegraph*'s report on our conference. It ran,

'Chimpanzees have souls – says Primate'

The 15 Tesla Problem

Office of the Dean

St Andrew's College
King George IV Bridge
Edinburgh EH1 1EE

ST ANDREW'S COLLEGE is an independent University College, geographically close to but not part of, the University of Edinburgh. We are often described as the 'Northern All Souls' (we're 'McCall Soles' in *Private Eye*) because like that splendid Oxford College, we have no undergraduates. We have only the academic staff, known as Dons, plus Postgraduates and Research Fellows from home and abroad, to the number of about 60. I'm actually never sure of the exact number since they pop in and out of existence in a relativistic and indeed quantum mechanical way. The College is superintended by myself as Dean, assisted by the Bursar, the Prebendary, the Warden and the Bedellus, all of whom sit on the 'Estaitis', an ancient Scots word for Council, dating back to our Foundation in 1561.

College is mercifully quiet at present, thanks to the summer break when most of the eccentrics who teach or research here are away on leave or disrupting conferences. That is, except those weirdest of our physicists, they of the AGL (the Anti-Gravity Lab). They have refused to leave, telling me yet again that they're on the verge of a breakthrough. If they'd break through into one of the parallel Universes they go on about, I'd be frankly delighted, given the mayhem here last week.

What happened it seems, is that one of them tripped over Schrödinger, the cat they keep in the AGL for quantum experiments. In falling, this clot desperately stuck his hand out and caught the 'Disarm!' lever of the lead shielding round the powerful 15 Tesla Magnetic field they use. Suddenly released, the field now blanketed King George IV Bridge which runs past the College. Confusingly, the Bridge is actually a major Edinburgh street. Anyway, before they tumbled to what was happening, the gigantic and invisible field, 15 times the strength of the Earth's own magnetic Field, had ensnared a passing Number 42 Stockbridge bus. I happened to be looking out from my study windows when to my astonishment I saw the now highly magnetised bus suddenly execute a swerving left turn and crash through the front door of the College. It charged into the atrium, demolishing the Mammoth skeleton before heading determinedly in the direction of the AGL. Thank God it was a single-decker… the bus passed through the staff canteen where it was joined by hundreds of flying knives, forks, blenders etc, all equally magnetic. Now looking like a giant porcupine, the thing finally came to rest in the women's restroom, scattering the occupants while powerfully attracting those wearing metallic underwear or surgical appliances. Before the Field could be switched off, it had also attracted or rather *tractored* into our entrance hall, a garbage truck, several automobiles and the ATM machine (with its contents) from the Bank of Edinburgh across the street.

I had to explain all this later to an *extremely* grumpy President who was staring at a bill from Lothian Buses for a new vehicle, while the Bank considers whether the abduction of its ATM, plus £25,500 in notes, constitutes armed robbery. The President has always regarded the AGL with the deepest suspicion since the antimatter explosion last year, despite the fact that they're one of our greatest revenue-earners. He'll get over it.

Right, that's all for today. I have now to attend a meeting with the Chinese Legation here – who are apparently incensed at an article in the *British Journal of Sport Archaeology* by our historian Dr David Wilkie. According to the Chinese, their game of *Chui Wan*, ('hit ball – with stick' in Mandarin) is the progenitor of Golf and dates from the Ming Dynasty, long before the game appeared at St Andrews or anywhere else in this country... according to Wilkie, however, it's the other way round. The game, says he, was actually brought to the Middle Kingdom from Scotland in 1421 by the Ming Emperor's squadron of ocean-going war-junks commanded by Admiral Zheng He. Apparently he, or rather He, came ashore at North Berwick with a squad of marines, interrupted a golf competition and grabbed clubs and balls before making off to the ship, pursued into the surf by the furious locals.

The fact that the 10th hole at the ancient North Berwick Golf Club is called 'Eastward Ho' (clearly a misprint for *He*) seems pretty conclusive – but we'll see.

The Guest in the Laundry Chute

Office of the Dean

St Andrew's College
King George IV Bridge
Edinburgh EH1 1EE

A MOST EMBARRASSING incident this morning. At about 7 a.m. the laundry staff in the basement heard muffled cries coming from a large heap of linen at the bottom of the College's laundry chute. Investigation revealed Emeritus Professor Sir Lionel Trelawney of Cambridge among the used bedding etc, still in evening dress and having apparently spent the night *in situ*.

A world authority on the pre-Socratic philosophers of Greece, Lionel gave the Bertrand Russell memorial Lecture here yesterday. His subject was that fiery pre-Socratic philosopher Empedocles of Agrigentum, the sage of Sicily who committed suicide in spectacular fashion by leaping into the *caldera* of Mt Etna. Lionel had finished with a memorable sally from the *History of Western Philosophy* by Bertrand Russell, who quotes an unnamed poet on the subject: 'Great Empedocles, that *ardent* soul, Leapt into Etna – and was roasted, whole!'

LAUNDRY CHUTE
A MUFFLED VOICE!
A SPALPEEN OR ANOTHER TOFF-MISFIT OR DEVIANT- NO DOUBT

Anyway, as a guest of College, old Lionel dined last
night at High Table with myself, the Rector, the Bursar
and the usual crowd of Dons and guests. He was in good
form, discoursing as usual upon the Empedoclean
Fragments. These I should point out are all that survive
of the sage's writings – not what remained of *him* post-
Etna. Having made a fair dent in our stocks of claret, he
went on to relish the College vintage port. His impish
sense of humour was well to the fore;

'Meiklejohn,' said he to his old friend, our Chair of
Epistemology, 'I think you should drink *less* port!'

'But why, Lionel?'

'Because, old boy, I've been watching you – and your
face is becoming dishtinctly fuzzy!'

And with that, amid the laughter, he departed to bed.

Next morning I was told of the remarkable discovery
in the laundry chute. Our guest bedrooms being on the
4th floor, I sent the Bedellus to fetch him, keen to
discover how on earth he had landed, literally, among
the bedding in the basement. Thankfully none the worse
for his adventures, he was shown into the Deanery;
whereupon it emerged that it was all *my* fault! As he's
nearly 90, I had indeed told him to use our new
Smythson Stairlift to reach his guest bedroom on the top
floor landing. However, I had apparently omitted to tell
him to read the stairlift's printed *Instructions* with due
diligence.

Now, the College's normally sedate stairlift also has a
Turbo setting which does the job at far higher speeds. A

standing joke in College is that it allows our aged Bursar to reach the top floor before forgetting what he was there for. Anyway, the *Turbo* setting requires application of a powerful brake to slow the thing down on its approach to its upper terminus. It's only used by our engineers and the younger Dons, all of whom are strictly charged that on leaving the stairlift, the Control handle *must* be returned from *Turbo* to *Standard*. This had not been done…

Dear old Lionel had apparently eased himself snugly on to the seat, pressed *Activate* – and found himself hurtling upstairs at alarming speed. His cries were unheard as he soared past the Labs on the 2nd floor, ascended beyond the Seminar Rooms on the 3rd and found himself rapidly approaching the 4th floor Terminus, unaware that the brakes were now urgently required. We even have a sign on the banister saying *BRAKE!* for just such an emergency but he was going far too fast to see it.

With hindsight, it was a mistake to position the 4th floor laundry-chute flap opposite the stairlift terminus. There was an almighty *BANG* as the seat crashed to a halt – unlike Lionel. Now obeying Newton's 1st Law of Motion, he continued straight across the landing until partially arrested by the chute's entrance flap. This opened to receive him and then closed again as he began an equally rapid descent, bouncing off the sides until coming mercifully to a soft landing four floors below on the linen pile. There, literally blanketed amid the bedding and sedated by the Port, he drifted into the arms of Morpheus until awakened by Mrs O'Malley our Irish laundry-lady.

The following conversation then ensued.

'Good morning, madam,' said the voice from the sheets, 'May I enquire if this is Sir Lionel Trelawney's room?

'Ah, go on with ye, sir. Sure, ye're Sir Trelawney himself!'

'Madam, I know who I *am* – I am enquiring if this is my *room!*'

'Dis is the sump of the linen chute sir. Jaysus, if it was yer shirt or yer knickers ye wanted washin', sure ye just leave them outside yer *door...!*'

EMERITUS PROF SIR LIONEL TRELAWNEY OF CAMBRIDGE CRACKS A JOKE

Coffee was served as I tendered our unreserved apologies for his lightning tour of our facilities.

'Don't mention it, old boy,' was the response, 'reminded me of being on the Cresta Run more than a few years back – and I had a softer landing than old Empedocles, what?'

The conversation turned inevitably to the Pre-Socratics, before veering off, predictably in the circumstances, to the adventures of Dons in strange academic surroundings. We exchanged stories of our colleagues' adventures abroad and concluded that the best of all concerned The Chancellor, no less, of a certain Oxbridge university. Having attended an academic meeting years ago in Russia, he was pursued home by a furious set of telegrams alleging that the fire which had consumed a wing of the accommodation block at the Soviet Academy of Sciences, had been traced to his bedroom. It had been caused, fumed the telegrams, by his lighted cigar, dropped during a vodka-fuelled slumber. Repairs would run into hundreds of thousands of Roubles – and the bill was coming his way.

'Absolutely outrageous', wrote back the Chancellor, 'A disgraceful calumny and unfounded allegation; and for two reasons:

One; I was stone cold sober.

Two; the bed was already on fire when I got into it...'

High Table Dining

Office of The Dean

St Andrew's College
King George IV Bridge
Edinburgh EH1 1EE

W ITH MOST OF the staff on summer vacation till the start of the Martinmas Term in early October, the College should be mercifully quiet. It is not. These days, like all academic centres with lecture halls and accommodation, we make serious money during Summer Vacation by hosting conferences and seminars. We also supply three venues for Edinburgh's astonishing – and now gigantic – Festival Fringe.

This latter activity has brought 'comedians' into College this year. The dress, language and general behaviour of these individuals is regarded by my colleagues as eccentric; a fact remarkable in an institution where the competition is already pretty fierce. However, more of the Fringe comedians' antics anon.

We were also privileged to have a visit from the distinguished Anglo-Greek philosopher Prof. Rocco Hector Simonides. He has kindly allowed me to reprint his subsequent article in the *Hellenic Philosophy Quarterly* describing Dinner at our High Table.

'Through the subdued roar of conversation, an insistent clink and ping of Sheffield knife on Edinburgh crystal permeated down to the lower reaches of the Great Hall. The pings sharpened in clarity as a tottering silence emerged. The Dons and Fellows of St Andrew's College leaned forwards or back and gazed up to High Table.

The Dean rose, unaware of his academic gown silently sweeping a large glass of Oloroso sherry into the capacious lap of the Rector.

'The Prebendary,' he announced, 'will ask Grace in the name of…'

'Christ!' shouted the Rector, recoiling as the first seepage of sherry reached his groin.

'Thank you, Rector,' said the Dean evenly, nodding to the tall dog-collared Prebendary now standing at the lectern.

The Prebendary closed his eyes and nodded to the Rector who banged his tuning–fork on the table, producing the pure B-flat in which the Prebendary habitually intoned his Graces. This, together with his use of Latin and his drop-down from B-flat to G for the last syllable of each line, led to an aura of monkish plainsong – and to mutterings of 'nascent Popery' from the Calvinists among the theologians present.

'*Gratias tibi agimus, Domine, pro Christo bo-no,*

Aquam qui in vinum mutaa-vit', intoned the Prebendary, giving *mutavit* a long '*aa*' and a powerful dying fall on the -*vit*.

'*Et pro his omnibus a quibus mox revertiee-tur.*'

Bowing to the Dean and High Table, the Prebendary swept back to his place down the hall. As he went, he bestowed a huge wink on his fellow classicists, followed by a pious deadpan to the quietly seething Calvinists.

'Did he *say* that?' said Yancey, a newly-arrived American Platonist to his neighbour, a table napkin held to his face, 'I do not *believe* he said that!'

'And what, precisely,' said Anstruther the philosopher drily, 'did he say *this* time? You have the Latin.'

'He actually said we should thank J.C. for turning the water into wine; and thank God for all of *us* who're about to turn it *back again*!'

Yancey stared at his neighbour; nothing at Princeton had prepared him for this.

'Excellent,' said Anstruther reaching for the wine with a grin at the others, 'We thus have an impossibility linked causally to an absolute certainty. Remind me to speak to him, *again*.'

Yancey gazed around him. It was all too sudden, coming at his first Dining-In. He told me that he had been cautioned back home by Dean Horowicz of Princeton that of all the University Colleges in all of Europe, St Andrew's was hard to match in terms of sheer eccentricity.

'You're goddam lucky to be going, boy,' Horowicz had said at their parting, ' I was there in the 60s for a year and learned more about ancient history just gazin' around, than in any goddam book. You've got two years. Use 'em!'

Yancey gazed up the hall from his lowly position well below the salt. Three long tables with Dons and Fellows facing each other ran lengthwise up Great Hall. They sprigged into High Table which lay transversely like a giant crossed 'T'. This contained the Dean, Bursar and Rector, plus other senior College officers and any visiting academic fireman deemed worthy of a place.

All the black–gowned luminaries at The High, as the top table is known, faced down the hall thus allowing the Dons an uninterrupted view of the eating and drinking habits of their betters – and *vice versa*. It also allowed a stream of comment from the older Dons who stoutly maintained the College's tradition of academic irreverence.

'Now, Dr Yancey of Princeton,' said Jack Anstruther, indicating The High, 'what, pray, is the difference between yonder black-gowned Dr Hamish Auchincloss and a *Diomedea melanophris*, the black-browed albatross?'

Yancey grinned. He already knew this format.

'I dunno. Go right ahead.'

'There is no difference. Both circle the world in a downwind direction and both are notoriously unstable, particularly when faced with a landing on the nest!'

Considerable hilarity followed this from our neighbours; we then learned that the large Professor of Gaelic Literature had recently returned to Edinburgh from yet another extended visit to Australia and New Zealand.

Whether due to jet-lag, duty-free whisky or both, the wandering academic eventually located his Morningside home, but tripped on tip-toeing into the darkness of the conjugal bedroom. In falling, he rammed and brought down the cage of Ossian the parrot whose screams awakened Mrs Auchincloss who activated her personal alarm before spraying her husband – and Ossian – with *Mace*®. Subsequent newspaper articles dwelt at considerable length with Ossian's fight for survival in, and noisy reluctance to leave, the A&E department of Edinburgh's Dickson Veterinary Institute. Had he been able to read the sign above the Dickson's General Public Dispensary he'd have put his beak to an ID (Immediate Discharge) form. The sign reads:

The Dickson Vet Institute

Veterinary Surgeons – and Taxidermists

(whatever happens, you'll get your pet back...)

In summary, dear colleagues, an academic sojourn to what the Scots are pleased to subtitle 'The Athens of the North' is not to be missed. Forget that Lord Elgin of our Marbles was one of them. Should you have a Scottish visitor here in Athens, be sure to comment that *its* subtitle is 'The Edinburgh of the South!'

Misprisions

Office of the Dean

St Andrew's College
King George IV Bridge
Edinburgh EH1 1EE

THERE WAS A serious debate last night at High Table over misprisions. What are they and where did they come from? What is a single and what a *double* misprision?

Its origin is apparently from Middle English, deriving from the Old French *mesprendre*, from *mes-* 'wrongly' + *prendre* 'to take'. The term is thus a 'mis-take'; no mistake about that.

Historically, advises the OED, a *misprision* is the deliberate 'concealment of one's knowledge of a treasonable Act or a Felony' – and was presumably punishable by imprisionment. The modern meaning, however, carries far less menace, being where one takes someone for someone else, a major mistake indeed.

Now, this is where it gets interesting and potentially hilarious. An SMP (single misprision) is where one party to a conversation is convinced that the other party is indeed someone else. The much rarer DMP (double misprision), on the other hand, is where *both* parties believe that the other is other than the one each thought the other was. Clear?

This happened to Churchill at one of his lunches during the War. At the beginning of each week his Private Secretary would present him with a list of personages who were in Town. The great man would then tick the names of six or so guests to be bidden to No 10. One day in 1941 he saw on the list, '*I. Berlin*'. Excellent, thought WSC. Tick! Sir Isaiah Berlin, the celebrated Oxford philosopher, had never met Churchill. He was then attached to our Embassy in Washington DC to help persuade the Cousins to join in the war; he must be home on leave...

Came the lunch. Berlin was seated next to the PM, by whom he was greeted warmly and congratulated on his contribution to War Effort. Was he just in from the States? Indeed he was, said Berlin, surprising Churchill with his powerful Brooklyn accent, obviously picked up to impress the locals. Now, the joy of a misprision is that the mistaken party, *convinced* of the other's identity, will override even the most obviously evidences to the contrary.

'Will Roosevelt get his third Term?' queried the PM.

'Well, *Ah'm* sure gonna vote for him,' said Berlin.

'Really? You've got a *Vote*...?'

'Sure. I'm a registered Democrat!'

Clearly, the Oxford Don had gone native.

Churchill's surprise was well founded. For 'I. Berlin,' his lunch companion, was not Sir Isaiah Berlin but Mr Irving of that ilk. Churchill was not entertaining the moralist author of *Two Concepts of Liberty* and the great biography of Karl Marx, he was entertaining the author of *Annie get your Gun* and *Everybody's doin' it, doin' it!* Still believing it *was* Sir Isaiah, Churchill then put to I. Berlin a serious of questions which the songsmith later retailed to his friends back in New York,

'He asks me all sorts of things about politics and philosophy and this kinda stuff, and I had to tell him straight, 'Prime Minister, I have *no* idea about any of this.'

'Incredibly modest chap, that Berlin,' said Churchill to Brendan Bracken later. 'I put to him what I thought were serious questions about all the subjects he'd written about – and d'you know what he said? He said he had absolutely *no* idea what I was talking about. The man's intelligence is obviously on a *completely* different plane...'

Misprisions may involve the mistaken identity of objects as well as persons. My formidable great-aunt Elizabeth was an authority on Sir William Wallace, the tragic hero of Scotland's 12th century War of Independence. That great book, *The Actes & Deedes of Schir Wm. Wallace, Knicht*, was lying as usual on a table beside her chair one day when her parish minister called for afternoon tea. The tome, calf-bound and bulky, does indeed look like the Bible – for which the Rev. MacKenzie promptly mistook it. Misprision!

'I am *so* pleased to observe, Miss Elizabeth,' said he, indicating the book, 'that you've been reading about our Saviour.'

'Indeed I have, minister. One of the greatest men who ever lived.'

'Indeed he was; and of course we must never forget that he was to suffer and die for all of us.'

'Indeed he did. His trial was a disgrace; and so was the barbarous death he suffered that same day, in London.'

'In... *London*?'

'Indeed.'

'Not in Jerusalem, then?'

'Of course not!'

There was another DMP involving, of all things, the condom that wasn't. A medical student taking his Final Examination was seated opposite two stern examiners across a table upon which lay a variety of *objets d'art* from the world of Obstetrics and Gynaecology. He was instructed to open a white cardboard box which contained a large 'Dreadnought' condom. Now, neither party was aware that prior to the examination, the room had been entered by an unknown practical joker. This person had opened the white box, extracted the said condom – and replaced it with a McVitie's chocolate digestive biscuit.

The student opened the box and peered in surprise at its contents. These were invisible to the examiners, one of whom said,

'Now, you recognise that object of course?'

'I do.'

'Would you agree that it has a definitive place in modern contraceptive practice?'

'Er, yes…'

'You don't sound too sure. What instructions would you give the patient regarding its application to the relevant member?'

'Patients should *not* apply it to their members. They should be advised that, *before* intercourse, it should be… consumed.'

'*Consumed?*'

'Yes, consumed. Preferably with tea.'

'Let *me* see that box…'

He passed.

The Decalogue

Office of the Dean

St Andrew's College
King George IV Bridge
Edinburgh EH1 1EE

THE COLLEGE remains relatively peaceful as we move through our summer vacation while hosting a parade of lucrative Conferences and Seminars, to the financial delight of the Bursar. We are most fortunate to be just a few hundred yards from the Royal Mile at the heart of what is now one of Europe's most popular cities for academic meetings.

However, the College's Martinmas Term, which begins the academic year, starts on 1 October, when we all return to work; that is, except my friend the deeply intellectual Prof. Abraham Rabbinowitz, my Head of Semitic Studies who, as you may already have surmised, is Jewish. Abe was in the Deanery this morning to tell me that 1 October may be the Feast of Martinmas and the first day of Term for *goyim* like me, but it is also the first day of *Sukkot* for orthodox Jews like him. Work is apparently forbidden as he and the family celebrate the first day of this 'Feast of Tabernacles'. These were apparently the flimsy dwellings occupied by his ancestors during the 40 years when they wandered around the Sinai desert before getting fed up and heading for Tel Aviv.

Now, I'm a huge admirer of Jewish humour and couldn't resist telling him about the alternative version of Exodus. This has Moses descending, from Mt Sinai *very* slowly, weighed down by two giant Tablets of granite. On these, the *Decalogue* (the Ten Commandments) had been incised, presumably in Hebrew, by YHWH the Tetragrammaton, from the Greek τετραγράμματον, 'four letters' (Jehovah to you).

'Hear me, O my people,' says Moses, 'I bring some good news and some bad news already. Which first do you want?'

'Oy vey, Moses!' cries his brother Aaron, 'Forty *years* we've been in this sodding desert. The *good* news give us first!'

'Right,' says Moses, holding up the Tablets, 'I've got him down to *Ten...*'

'And the bad news?'

'Adultery's still in...'

Thinking of *The Decalogue*, antecedents for which exist in Hittite literature by the way, it features in a present I received from my opposite number at All Souls College, our academic 'twin'. This gem is *The Oxford book of Oxford*, edited by the extraordinary Jan (formerly James) Morris, author of the trilogy *Pax Britannica* and a terrific writer. Anyway, an Oxford undergraduate is undergoing an oral Theology exam was asked how one should regard the Decalogue. Not at all sure what the Decalogue actually *was*, the student cannily replied,

'With reverence, Master, and not unmixed with awe.'

'Excellent, I quite agree.'

As is well known, there are 12 tribes of Judah which comprise the Jewish people. Legend has it, however, that there was once a 13th tribe, now lost to history. It was once thought that it might be the Falashas, a tribe in the Semien Mountains of northern Ethiopia who had been observed to be observing Jewish observances. This observation caused considerable excitement in Tel Aviv; the Falashas were airlifted to Israel and feted as returning members of the original diaspora.

Alas, when their DNA, and specifically their Y chromosome polymorphic markers, were checked, it turned out that they were an African people. At some point in their remote past they had adopted circumcision, observance of *Shabbat* etc, possibly through contact with some wandering ancient Hebrews. Mind you, they had also clearly adopted a facility in business, their removal to *Eretz Yisrael* taking them from poverty to relative affluence in a modern state.

Then there was Arthur Koestler. Back in the '70s he sensationally alleged, in *The Thirteenth Tribe* that the Ashkenazim (European Jews) are not descended from the Israelites of antiquity. No, they were Khazars, a Turkic people originating between the Black Sea and the Caspian. Koestler's hypothesis was that the Khazars converted to Judaism in the 8th century and migrated westwards into

Eastern Europe. This brought down on Koestler a storm of abuse from the ivory towers; anthropologists, ethnologists, philologists and other -ologists combining to rubbish the very *thought* that the most successful branch of Jewry might actually be... Turks! The book, however, met with support here at home from Sir Fitzroy MacLean: that remarkable Highland chieftain, soldier, diplomat and author of *Eastern Approaches*. Fitzroy thought that Koestler was right, but the irony is that Fitzroy was wrong. Wrong because, I suggest, that he himself was one of the *actual* 13th tribe – the Scots!

Scotland is one of the very few countries in Europe that never had a *pogrom*, England certainly did. Five million Scots live in Scotland with 15 million in the diaspora; five million Jews are in Israel and 15 million elsewhere. We have the same passion for business innovation, finance and education. Only the US competes with Scotland and Israel in the number of graduates produced per head of population; and all three countries head the premier division for academic papers published. On the literary front, was the national bard of Scotland not Rabbie Burns? My own *yarmulke* or skull cap, a present from my friend Dr David Shapiro, has ט-*13 שבט יהודי** embroidered on the margin. It all fits, as does my *yarmulke*, which caps it all.

Some years ago, arriving in Jerusalem to give a lecture at the Hebrew University's Ein Kerem campus, I was met by Prof. Avi Rahamimov, then the Dean of the Medical School.

'*Shalom*!' said he, 'Come to my office at once for coffee and an argument.'

'What about?'

'Who cares! The best arguments on *earth* are between Scots like you – and *Sabras* like me. Get on with it. Say anything and I'll profoundly disagree.

'Ok, you asked for it. Right; Jews are *smart*...!

'Say something else!'

We *have* to be related; but mark you, no-one is getting a sight of, let alone getting their hands on, my Y chromosome...

* *Tribe of Judah* (No13)

Richard Porson MA

Office of the Dean

St Andrew's College
King George IV Bridge
Edinburgh EH1 1EE

I REALISED A long-standing ambition this Whitsun Term as organiser and co-Chair of a College symposium on the state of Greek and Latin scholarship in our Universities. It was cheekily titled:

Classical Scholarship – an Antique Roadshow?

As the Symposium loomed, I exercised my right of *Ius Decanii*, our College's version of *Droit de Seigneur*. Dating from 1562, this is the privilege of the Dean to give a Lecture at *any* conference held in the College. This license operates whatever the subject and, most importantly, whatever the level of the Dean's ignorance of it.

However, the Classics being a first love from my schooldays, I was on sure ground with a paper with the suitably imposing title:

The Life & Times of Richard Porson Esq.,

Now, I have long been an admirer of the truly extraordinary Porson. Eccentric even by Trinity College standards, he was appointed Professor of Greek at Cambridge in 1792 and was still in the Chair in 1808 when he crossed the Styx from, of all places, the St Martin's Lane workhouse in London. The sheer contrast between Porson's brilliant classical scholarship and his Dionysian devotion to the bottle and resulting social mayhem, had always intrigued me. So has his chaotic appearance, photographic memory and his ability to identify any liquid even *likely* to contain alcohol.

At some future date I shall regale readers of the *Diary* with Porson's advances in our understanding of Homer's *Iliad* and the plays of Euripides through his emendations to the ancient texts. But for the present, let me confine myself to the man's lifestyle which for eccentricity is probably unequalled in the history of Academia – a field in which the competition is particularly fierce.

Born in a Norfolk village in 1759, the son of the parish clerk, Porson showed early promise and was funded to Eton by the local squire. He then had a spell as tutor to the son of a landowner on the Isle of Wight, but was dismissed after being discovered drunk and unconscious in a turnip field. At Cambridge, his progress in the Classics was meteoric. His MA of 1775 was followed by a

Fellowship at Trinity and then promotion to the Chair of Greek. He edited the tragedies of Euripides and Aeschylus and the comedies of Aristophanes. He worked on the lexicons of Photius and Suidas and propounded Porson's Law of scansion, still in use today. He was unsurpassed in correcting classical manuscripts whose transcriptional errors had accumulated down the centuries. He was, in a word, astonishing. Here at St Andrew's, among our weirdo Fellows, mad-cap Dons, late-sitters and high-kickers we neither have, nor ever have had, anything quite like him. More's the pity...

He would drink *anything*. The famous portraitist John Hoppner RA (1758–1810) was once residing in a cottage outside London when one evening his friend Porson unexpectedly arrived. Hoppner apologised that he could not offer him dinner as his wife Phoebe had gone to Town, prudently taking the key of the wine closet. Porson, however, declared that he would be content with mutton chops and beer from the neighbouring alehouse and would stay to dine. During the evening Porson said,

'I am certain that Mrs Hoppner keeps a bottle for her private drinking in her own bedroom. Pray, Hoppner, see if you can lay hands on it.' His host confidently assured him that Mrs Hoppner had no such secret store of drink, but Porson was absolutely insistent that a search be made. A bottle was then discovered in the lady's apartment (to the considerable surprise of Hoppner), whereupon Porson drained the contents, pronouncing it the best Gin he had tasted for some time.

Next day, Hoppner, somewhat out of temper with his wife, informed her coldly that Porson had drunk every drop of her concealed drink supply.

'Drunk every drop of it?' cried Phoebe, 'My God, it was the spirit for the *lamps!*'

The philologist John Horne Tooke MP (1736–1812) was a friend of the bucolic classicist, once observing dryly,

'Porson? He would drink *ink* rather than not drink at all.'

Dining with him in Richmond Buildings and aware that Porson had not been to bed for three nights, Tooke confidently expected him to leave at a tolerably early hour. Porson, however, kept both of them up the whole night drinking. As dawn broke, the exhausted Tooke, now in utter despair of getting shot of him, said,

'Dr Porson, pray excuse me. I am engaged to breakfast with a friend at a coffee-house in Leicester Square.'

'Splendid,' replied Porson, 'Tooke, I shall go with you.'

Accordingly he did so. However, soon after weaving their way to the coffee-house, the terrified MP contrived to slip out and escape. Stumbling home at speed, he shouted to his servants to lock the house and *not* to let Porson in even if (as was to happen) he should attempt to batter down the door.

'A man,' observed a shaken Tooke, 'who could sit up *four* successive nights, might have sat up *forty*...'

Porson would indeed drink absolutely anything. He was once sitting with a fellow guest in the London Temple apartment of a mutual friend who was ill and confined to bed upstairs. A servant came into the room, sent down by his master for a bottle of embrocation which had been on the chimney-piece.

'Drank it an hour ago,' said Porson.

He had a truly wicked sense of humour in the dry, laconic and devastating style of his contemporaries Horace Walpole and John Wilkes Booth.

The historian and fellow classical scholar Edward Gibbon (1737–1794) wrote to Porson, requesting the pleasure of his acquaintance. Porson accordingly called upon the older man who received him with every kindness. In the course of conversation Gibbon said,

'Dr Porson, having read my *History of the Decline & Fall of the Roman Empire*, I should be obliged by any remarks upon it which might suggest themselves.'

Porson was highly flattered by this, regarding the book as one of the finest literary productions of the century. Although in the habit of quoting long passages from it, he was also heard to say,

'There could be *no* better exercise for a schoolboy than to translate a page of it into English...'

In contrast to the grave classicists of his own time – and indeed mine – in terms of humour Porson was a dolmen on a barren plain. He was an epigrammatist to rank with Martial and a wit to rival Wilkes. For example, in 1805 the future poet laureate Robert Southey brought out his epic poem *Madoc*, a work regarded (correctly) by Porson as five thousand lines of uninterrupted, interminable tedium. Of it, said the proud author,

'My Madoc has brought a mere trifle financially, but

let me tell you, it will be read when Homer and Virgil are forgotten!'

Said Porson,

'Indeed it will – but not until then...'

The Dean at Oxford

Office of the Dean

St Andrew's College
George IV Bridge
Edinburgh EH1 1EE

Pray excuse the shaky writing and even shakier grammar, but this is written on a *very* shoogly express train between Kings Cross and the Edinburgh terminus named after Sir Walter Scott's first novel. One of the joys of academia is descending on fellow academics elsewhere and subjecting them to the delight of one's company, the results of one's latest research and the implied superiority of one's home institution. This was not easy at Oxford. This very week the place was rated, along with Cambridge, MIT, Harvard, Caltech and somewhere else, as among the Top Ten institutions anywhere on the planet.

A day or so ago, I spent a most profitable afternoon at the 'Bod', the Bodleian Library, examining manuscripts of the poet Robert Burns. However, I first had to be issued with a reader's ticket, or 'Bodcard'. This involved attending the Bod's Admissions Office in The Broad (Oxford's accurately named Broad St), where I was examined, photographed and scolded for not bringing a letter from my Dean.

'But I *am* the Dean!'

'That is not the *point!*'

This pointless discussion ended with my being required to visually identify myself. I was strongly tempted to use the famous Peter Ustinov response. This involves pulling out a small mirror, gazing at it intently for a few moments, and saying firmly,

'Yep. This is me.'

I was then required to read, from a card, a promise not to deface, annotate, tear up, or otherwise destroy any book or manuscript in the Bod – and never, *ever*, to set fire to it.

I left the Admissions Office full of scholarly rectitude, determined not to incendiarise anything remotely Bodlike. Outside, I paused to look at the splendid busts of Roman Emperors which ring the Sheldonian Theatre next door. I was checking for beads of sweat upon their stony brows, a routine activity among classicists. As described by Beerbohm in his delightful *Zuleika Dobson*, the appearance of imperial perspiration on the brows of the said Emperors is a hallucination brought on by drinking too much old Falernian, or reading too much Mommsen.

Later, dinner in Trinity was a delight. Who should be also there but Prof. John Nelson, our own Head of Classics who had been inserting Cicero's *Tusculan Disputations* into the undergraduate mind. Oxford of course has no students, only undergraduates who do not 'study' anything; they 'read' it.

All Souls, our own sister College at Oxford, doesn't even have undergraduates, only Dons, Postgrads and Research Fellows like us; and just as well, for students are a menace. Every year I am a year older, while every year they are exactly the same age. It's intolerable.

However, they do supply good anecdotage for dinner at High Table. At Trinity I heard of the tall, aristocratic-looking undergraduate who was halted, well past midnight, weaving down The High (Oxford's High Street) by a Proctor and his bulldog. Proctors are officers of the University charged with enforcing discipline among the student body – no easy task.

This confrontation produced a classic exchange, for our undergraduate was not alone… On his arm was a woman who would have formerly been described as 'of uncertain virtue' in England – and in the *patois* of Edinburgh as, 'Ane Hure off the streetis'. However in these PC days such individuals must be categorised as 'SW' for sex workers.

Anyway, the Proctor halted the pair, addressing the student with the traditional – and feared – Challenge:

'Your name and College, Sir?'

'I… am Julian Crutchley-Shmythe of Merton.'

'Indeed? And who is this woman?'

'Thish… is my *sister*.'

'Come on Sir, let us not play games. She is a common, and I may say, a notorious prostitute!'

'I *know*. Mummy's absolutely *steaming* about it!'

I went on to London to attend the Lord Mayor's

Banquet at Guildhall, a splendid white–tie bash enlivened, for those who saw it, by David Cameron's dress shirt. This object was either too small or the PM was putting on weight, because right after the consommé had been served, *Pop!* and out flew two pearl studs from his shirt-front. We were then treated to a prolonged stud reinsertion routine, it clearly being a night off for No.10's stud manager.

He's lucky that we don't have to wear the old board-stiff shirt fronts nailed down with studs, which caused Bertie Wooster such grief. Our hero would be doing justice to an insolent Chablis while making progress with the Hon. Virginia Shagwell, when *Boing!* – up would fly the shirt-front and down would go his chances.

The LM's Banquet was enlivened by an excellent speech by the outgoing Archbishop of Canterbury, the Most Rev Dr Rowan Williams. A truly intellectual Primate, his calm acceptance of the virgin conception, gestation and birth, must be one of the epiphanies of the century. As I observed to our moral philosophy class yesterday, citing the divine David Hume,

'If any man advises me that his mother was, and is, a virgin; that his father was, and is, a ghost; and furthermore that he had been dead and buried for several days before our conversation, I immediate ask myself,

"Does this gentleman think I came up the street in a wheelbarrow?"'

New College

Office of the Dean

St Andrew's College
King George IV Bridge
Edinburgh EH1 1EE

THE COLLEGE remains officially on vacation till the commencement of Martinmas Term on Monday 1 October, but the Dons and the Research Fellows are now beginning to straggle back to Edinburgh. I went to a most interesting meeting last night just down the road from us at New College which perches on top of The Mound. Properly the *Earthen* Mound, this is a colossal ramp carrying a road which snakes up from Princes Street, the city's main thoroughfare, up to the ridge on which stands the Old Town of Edinburgh. The Mound was thrown up in the early 19th century with several million tons of earth excavated to lay the foundation of the buildings of the New Town.

New College is effectively the University's Faculty of Divinity, its entry court featuring a gigantic bronze statue of John Knox. Bible in hand and arm raised in declamation, the general impression it conveys to visitors is one of unrelieved menace. Heaven alone knows what he'd have made of the *graffito* recently discovered on a wall behind the College. Probably the work of a divinity undergraduate blessed, or perhaps cursed, with an heretical sense of humour, it featured that most intriguing of the *Beatitudes* from the New Testament:

> Blessed are the meek, for they shall inherit the Earth

Sprayed on the wall, in a very neat hand, was the message:

We *will* inherit the Earth, so we will. Ok !
Signed: The Meek
(If it's all right with you...)

New College was where the Scottish Parliament had its temporary home when it reconvened in 1999 after nigh on 300 years of recess. On that occasion, with the Queen present, Sheena Wellington memorably sang, 'A Man's a

Man, for a' That', Burns' great anthem for the Common Man which famously reminds peers, prelates and assorted popinjays that their rank is only the *stamp* on the golden Guinea piece. What really counts is what lies beneath that stamp; the true metal of the people.

Thinking of our revived Parliament meeting first at New College, reminds me that it did so because the new Parliament House at Holyrood was yet unfinished, while going spectacularly over budget. This caused considerable amusement south of Hadrian's Wall. Our neighbours delight in tales of our canniness such as the Aberdonian who accidentally dropped not a Guinea but a 50p piece over the balcony of his 12th floor flat. Down he went to retrieve it – only to be laid out cold when it hit him on the head.

Anyway, during the furore over the cost of Holyrood, I happened to be visiting All Souls College at Oxford, our sister College. In their senior common room a newspaper was lowered to reveal one of their oldest and most aristocratic Fellows. In tones which made Prince Charles sound like a welder, said he,

'Ah, Dean! It says here in the *Telegraph* that you Jocks, on a budget of £40 million, have gone through £450 million, building this Parliament in Edinburgh. That's a cost overrun of 1000 per cent! Isn't that, shall one say, rather un-*Jock-like*? ' Much laughter greeted this brilliant sally.

I went over to him, saying,

'Charles, you're right; there's no denying it. And

what's more, I can tell you, in strict confidence mind, that it's even worse than you think…'

'Oh really?'

'Yes, it's *your* money!'

Anyway, that's quite enough of politics for now. I have to be careful here, being the Dean of a college whose Dons and Fellows represent the most extraordinary spectrum of political colours. This ranges from the deep blue, indeed almost ultraviolet of Dr Sam Yancey, our Roosevelt Fellow and a mouthpiece for the neo-con Tea Party back home. Yancey is still pondering why his Party seems to be known in Edinburgh as the 'You'll have *had* your Tea Party.'

One day I'll tell him.

Deep in the infra-red at the opposite end of the spectrum, is the philosopher Prof. Angus McKittrick who fascinates me by combining great personal charm with being a resolutely doctrinaire anarchist. Angus does not recognise the existence of myself as Dean, or the College, or the University, or indeed the United Kingdom. Mark you, his refusal to recognise objects of authority has its lighter side. Arrested for refusing to recognise (i.e. pay) the Toll Charges on the Forth Bridge some years ago, he was being escorted up the steps into Dunfermline Sheriff Court by a local PC.

'I do not,' shouted Angus, '*recognise* this Court!'

'Neither do I,' said the Constable, 'It must have been repainted!'

Thankfully, however, he appears to accept the existence

of the Universe, but only on the grounds that it is essentially anarchic and has been, well, just *there* forever.

To the bemusement of our astrophysicists, he rejects the km as a fiendish crypto-theist device to imply a Creator. Last year he gave a memorable and (to me) hilarious lecture titled, 'Exploding the Big Bang' in which the Bang's proponents came in for some rough handling for their 'scientific insolence'. The Bang itself got a hammering for leaving no clue to its nature save the CMB (Cosmic Microwave Background). This is the silent snowstorm on the TV screen when consciousness returns at 3.00 a.m. on the Deanery couch after a heavy night at High Table.

Angus' lectures are hugely popular for being themselves anarchic. No chairman is permitted and there is no Q&A at the end, since that smacks of structure. Instead, from the very start he conducts a verbal fire-fight with the barracking, interrupting and delighted audience. Well, it takes all types to make the world, and thank God I'm not one of them.

Tomorrow sees the pre-term meeting of *Estaitis*, the College Council, known to Angus as the Supreme Soviet. There I'll be joined by the Senior Tutor, the Bursar, Warden and the Bedellus. We'll start the business with a prayer by the Prebendary, the Rev. Dr Hector Stuart, DD, who will enjoin us to seek guidance from the Almighty – or whatever it was that triggered the Big Bang.

He will then go down to New College with a mop and pail – to wipe out '*The Meek…*'

Scott and the Aussies

Office of the Dean

St Andrew's College
King George IV Bridge
Edinburgh EH1 1EE

THE COLLEGE IS still in Long Vacation until
Martinmas Term begins the new academic year on
1 October. Meanwhile I have been communing with
the spirit of Sir Walter Scott as advance copies of my
abridgement of his classic *Ivanhoe* go out to reviewers.
The central problem with Scott today is the hardback
covers of his books; they're just too far apart.

What I have done is to conserve the thundering
storyline of *Ivanhoe* while jettisoning the mass of
extraneous matter around the plot which expanded the
original to a colossal 195,000 words. Overboard have
gone thousands of commas and more colons than any of
my surgical colleagues remove in a clinical lifetime.
Conserved, however, are Scott's superb evocation of the
sights, sounds, smells and conflicts of 12th Century
England in the reign of Richard *Coeur de Lion*. Now at
95,000 words, the book is the length of a modern novel
and will hopefully appeal to the younger audience for
whom Scott has appeared, well, just too long.

The book was launched at the new Visitor Centre at Scott's Borders home of home of Abbotsford, near Melrose. The big house itself was re-opened by the Queen in June 2013 after a multi-million pound refit and is now just as much a Borders treasure as was its late owner, the 'Wizard of the North'.

I travelled to and from the Borders with an Australian friend from Sydney University. This was most helpful in three ways. Firstly, good conversation eats up the miles. Secondly, it triggered memories of his country to which I first went, newly graduated in medicine, as Ship's Surgeon on the P&O liner *Canberra*. I would return to Australia much later as Turnbull Scholar to the University of Melbourne. Thirdly, I have always been interested in the speech patterns of our antipodean cousins. These are brilliantly illustrated in that linguistic classic *Let's talk Strine*. Published in the mid-'60s by Alastair Ardoch Morrison, a good Scottish name, the book anthologised his humorous column on Australian speech in *The Sydney Morning Herald* under the pseudonym Affabeck Lauder * (an even better Scots name.)

Legend has it that the idea came from a book-signing in Sydney by that great Edinburgh-born novelist Muriel Spark. As usual on such occasions, she was seated at a desk in a bookshop as a queue of customers approached to give their names and have their copies autographed and dedicated. Eventually a young lady approached and laid a copy before Ms Spark who looked up, pen in hand.

'Emma Chissit,' said the customer.

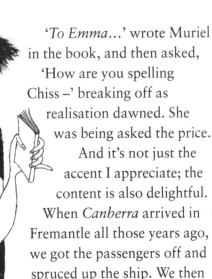

Emma

'*To Emma...*' wrote Muriel in the book, and then asked, 'How are you spelling Chiss –' breaking off as realisation dawned. She was being asked the price. And it's not just the accent I appreciate; the content is also delightful. When *Canberra* arrived in Fremantle all those years ago, we got the passengers off and spruced up the ship. We then ran the lines ashore to receive TV in our Wardroom, the officers' mess. On came the Australian Broadcasting Corporation's morning News and with it the Junior Minister of the Environment. He was to give his reaction to the sensational discovery, off the west coast of Australia, of a colony of a wallaby variant – let's call it the Simpson's wallaby. These marsupials were thought to have been hunted out generations ago, yet here they were, adults and joeys all hopping happily about.

'G'day,' boomed the Minister to the nation, 'All of us owe a bonzer debt of gratitude for the rip-snorter discovery that this animal's still aloive and well. The Government, believe me, will now make absolutely bloody certain, that the Simpson's wallaby *never* becomes extinct agyne...'

All that said, this College has benefited mightily down the years from the Australian colleagues who have spent time with us. Their inbuilt ability to take wry sideways look at the habits and customs of the Old Country and to call a spade a spyde has been a refreshment to us all. Long may it be so.

*Alphabetical Order (!)

Saints & Sinners

Office of the Dean

St Andrew's College
King George IV Bridge
Edinburgh EH1 1EE

THE COLLEGE IS now fully back in action for our Martinmas Term which lasts for ten weeks, with a break in late December for Yuletide. In accordance with our Constitution of MDLXI (1561), we do not recognise let alone observe Christmas, a Victorian import with until recently little place in the Scottish psyche. But more of our Yuletide Festival anon.

One of the pleasures of the Deanship is the Deanery on the top floor of College. Here I can work in peace, interview candidates, dismiss malefactors and generally run the show. Neither the Bursar, nor the Rector or even the Prebendary comes in here without an invitation. The Deanery is my private domain and comprises my study, ensuite bedroom *cum* dressing room and the Executive Office, all of these lying behind and hence protected by the outer offices housing the Secretariat.

The latter is my anti-tank ditch and rampart, or rather my Siegfried Line, across which none may pass without the approval of my splendid German secretary/PA.

Compared to this lady, Cerberus, the three-headed dog and gate-guardian of Hades, was a pussycat. Baroness Grimhilde von Reichenau-Strelitz, named after the Queen of the Gibichungs in Wagner's *Ring Cycle*, handles all my arrangements. Without Grimhilde, my life would be frankly a shambles. However, thanks to her imposition of strict Teutonic discipline, I somehow keep both myself and the College going.

However, I'm allowed out from time to time to represent College, one of the extracurricular events this week being the extraordinary Saints & Sinners luncheon over in Glasgow. The S&S comprises 100 individuals from all areas of industry, the arts and show-business who raise a phenomenal amount of money for Good Causes, while having a hilarious time doing so. The Scottish Club is the only offspring of the London parent S&S, itself the daughter of a now defunct New York institution.

These lunches are not for the faint-hearted. Grimhilde knows from experience to put absolutely *nothing* in the diary until the day after an S&S occasion and that my telephone and email facilities in the Deanery are not to be enabled until after my 'Bertie Wooster' (a restorative) the following morning.

The parent London S&S Club is a gem, populated by many of the great and good of the entertainment world. Years ago they asked me to partner Robert Runcie in the speeches at their 50th Anniversary Dinner at the Savoy. Unmissable! Down to London I went.

The first astonishment of many that evening, came on meeting the great man. Runcie was then Archbishop of Canterbury, a classical scholar, a war hero with an MC from the battlefields of Normandy to prove it and a great wit. He gave a splendid speech on the subject of sainthood, while proudly sporting a *red* carnation. I should perhaps point out that on entering the River Room that evening, one was offered the choice of red or white carnation as a buttonhole. The choice was meant to reflect whether one saw oneself as a Saint (white) or not...

'I see Your Grace wears the red.'

'It is my sacred duty to show solidarity with poor, miserable sinners such as myself!'

To my great surprise it transpired that the head of the Church of England was a Scot and, like your humble servant, from Ayrshire. I told him that his mellifluous, sibilant High Church tones were not exactly those of the Ayrshire recalled from a Prestwick childhood.

'Ah, but you see, my father – an engineer with Glenfield & Kennedy in Kilmarnock – was posted to Liverpool. And so, like the exiled Israelites in Psalm 137, I was born by the waters of Babylon – only in my case, the Mersey!'

Back at College I looked up 'Runcie' in *Black's Dictionary of Scottish Surnames* and right enough, there it was; the origin of the surname lay in Aberdeenshire. He certainly had the old Scots persistence, not least when our table was visited by 'J.A.K.', John Jackson, the celebrated cartoonist of the *London Evening Standard* and another famous wag.

'Ah, Jack,' says the Archbishop, 'now tell me; how on earth does this Club *determine* whether a new member is a Saint or a Sinner? We at the C of E have wondered how to do it for 500 years.'

'Easy,' says Jackson, 'we have a question we put to the new member.'

'And what is that *crucial* question?'

'We ask him: would you make love to a consenting 16-year-old?'

'But how does that distinguish them?'

'Well, a Saint will say '*No!*' while a Sinner will say, 'er... a 16-year-old *what...*?''

The London Saints & Sinners Christmas Lunch, also at the Savoy, is one of the hottest tickets of the Yuletide. Carols are sung – but with the words altered by Sir Tim Rice to reflect the political issues of the day e.g.

'Hark, the herald Angels sing,
N. Farage is up for King...!'

It was at that lunch in 2003, just a few months before his death, that I heard Peter Ustinov in person for the first, and last, time. Simply the very best after-lunch or dinner speaker this country has produced, he had it all: four languages; all the various accents for his superb mimicry; and that rare combination of brevity of language with breadth of expression.

He spoke of that fearful summer of 1940 and told of a 'pillbox', a concrete emplacement with a firing slit, on the south coast of England in which the then Private Ustinov waited, nervously, for the German mass invasion.

He shared that pillbox with Private Goldstein, a Jewish bespoke tailor from Warsaw, marooned in London by the invasion of his homeland. They were certainly ready for the *Wehrmacht*; not only did they have a rifle, they also had several rounds of ammunition. They also had a major communications problem. Goldstein could only speak Polish, Yiddish and German; while Ustinov was fluent in Russian, French, German and English. This meant that the only common language among these two British Army warriors, was German...

But that's another story.

Public Transport

Office of the Dean

St Andrew's College
King George IV Bridge
Edinburgh EH1 1EE

THERE SEEMS NO end to the public's thirst for being harangued. This Candlemas Term, I have given three lectures in widely different locations and on equally disparate subjects: 'The Enlightenment' to the University; on 'The Humour of Golf' to a Charity Day at Muirfield Links; and 'James Boswell' to the Carlyle Society. Disparate activities, especially if novel, are apparently useful in staving off the onset of dementia. Of course we should all do crosswords, particularly GK ones; play bridge; have a noontime siesta; eat blueberries till we sprout leaves and chuck out the tofu. But wait; there's a new idea about.

We had a lecture on the subject of Alzheimer's this week in College from an American professor of neuroscience. He later gave me a pat on the back for, unwittingly, doing the right thing; my varied harangues apparently help to keep the old pre-frontal cortex ticking over.

Talking to a rapt audience of ageing but wide-awake Dons, he told us that he advocates, above all, doing things *for the very first time*, as we get older. Apparently

varying one's routine and doing familiar things in a novel fashion is helpful in conserving the neural network. Thus we should brush our teeth with the non-dominant hand, inspect the family album upside down, shop at an ethnic market using *sign* language – and wear thick mittens when driving.

Apparently all this creates new pathways in the brain, clears out the cobwebs and stimulates the *hippocampus* ('horse-racetrack' in Greek) where the memory storage occurs. We have been using the MRI machine in our Sanatorium to look for HE (Hippocampal Enlargement) among our Dons. None has been found so far, but we did pick up a case or two of Trypanosomiasis. The scanning was interrupted by an operative of the Healthy & Safe Executive who made the mistake of entering

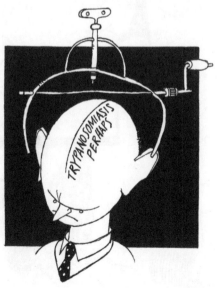

without permission from the formidable Sister Bronwen, our head nurse. He left, clearing the barrier in the atrium at a single bound. That London cabbies have unusually large ones, *hippocampoi* that is, was found by our colleagues at University College Hospital in London. Measuring the size of the cabby *hippocampus* using MRI (Magnetic Resonance Imaging), they found it to be bulging, presumably with 'The Knowledge'. This is their

three-dimensional mental map of the city's 12,000 streets and is mandatory. No knowledge, no licence.

In contrast, London bus drivers have wee ones. Presumably this is because they only need to memorise a few unalterable routes and are spared garbled instructions from capricious and sometimes legless passengers.

All this will doubtless lead to a new version of the old cabby routine;

'University 'ospital? Righto, guv... I'd that MRI on the back of me 'ead once...'

The next test should be of course to study the cerebral racetrack size of Edinburgh tram drivers who don't have to weave in and out of traffic, they only to have to stop and start, besides hooting at cyclists trapped on the rails.

Come to think of it, we're all trapped in the rails... one is reminded of the old Limerick on the subject of divine predestination:

> There once was a man who said 'Damn!'
>   I've just realised that I am
> A being that moves in predestinate grooves,
>   I'm not even a bus... I'm a Tram!

Trams, with cowbells attached to scare off citizens, started rolling along Princes St in June 2014. I remember fishing out my Senior Bus Pass wondering if it was tram-enabled. It was.

'Are you thus an OAP, Dean?' said the Bursar as I peered at the plastic.

'Certainly not, Bursar,' I retorted, 'and you can drop that grossly un-PC title. The term is SC – for Senile Citizen!'

I can leap on to a No. 42 omnibus outside the College here on George IV Bridge and be taken home free to my eyrie in India Place or indeed anywhere in Scotland. The one problem with the bus pass is that you *have* to go where the bus goes.

Alas, it has always been thus. When the (horse-drawn) Omnibus was introduced to London in the 1880s, Lord Brabazon, a delightfully eccentric Irish peer, first heard about it over dinner at the Carlton Club. Much later that night, he weaved out into St James' St and confronted an approaching omnibus, bringing the neighing horses to an abrupt halt with a swish of his blackthorn stick. Said he to the Conductor:

'I say, fellow, is thish the so-called Omnibush?'

'Yes, m'lord.'

'Splendid.' He climbed aboard. '21 Cadogan Square, thank you.'

The Brabazons were not born to travel publicly. His father Colonel John Arthur Henry Moore-Brabazon or 'Bwab' as he was known around town, could not say his 'Rs'. Neither was he *au fait* with public transport. This was a pity since the family 'Coach & Six' with its horses, coat-of-arms and liveried postilions, had had to be sold to mollify the creditors.

Down at Aldershot with his Regiment, he heard from a brother officer of the Guards that a 'railway' now connected the famous garrison town with London, whither he was headed on leave.

'A w*ailway*? Where does it awwive?'

'King's Cross, I believe.'

'Wight!'

At the new Aldershot station there followed a classic exchange with the Station Master on foot – and Bwab, up on his charger.

'I say, fellow, where's the London twain?'

'I'm afraid it's gone, Colonel.'

'Gorn? Gorn where?'

'Why, to London sir.'

'Well don't just *stand* there, fellow; bwing another!'

The Big Bang – and Chimps

Office of the Dean

St Andrew's College
King George IV Bridge
Edinburgh EH1 1EE

THE COLLEGE's Martinmas Term traditionally ends with the two-day Winter Symposium which this year was on 'Evolution' – and what a Christmas cracker it turned out to be...

Since our range of College disciplines stretches across the Humanities and the Sciences, I decided that the Symposium would not be limited to the evolution of *H. sapiens*. We would also take in the evolution of our planetary home and, what the hell, the Cosmos itself.

To this end, we began appropriately with a paper on the origin of the Universe and to give it, up stepped our Head of Astrophysics, Prof. Albert Braithwaite. Known predictably in College as 'Big Bang Bertie', as much for his volcanic temper as his subject, Albert treated us to an explosive review of the Bang. He wound up with a speculation on the vexed question of the big question of its causation. What – or *Who* – had let it off?

'Given that it is impossible to prove a negative,'

shouted Bertie over an ominous growing hubbub in the Great Hall, 'the bang-button could have been pressed, or the touch-paper lighted, by God, *or* by a focus group of Gods, *or* by God-knows-what *entities* acting on a Divine mandate, or even by a renegade God acting on a *whim*!'

I groaned inwardly when I heard this, because I knew what would be coming. And come it did. Bertie had triggered a nuclear firefight. With temperatures approaching that of the Bang itself, our Theologians in the Red Corner collided with our resident militant atheists under Dr Angus McKittrick in the Blue. It reminded me of the matter/antimatter explosion in the Anti-Gravity Lab last year which blew out every window

in the streets around; only it was louder. I still marvel at the ability of an event 13.7 *billion* years ago to reduce learned academics to apoplexy.

'Atheist!' cried the theologians.

'*Thank* you!' shouted McKittrick, 'Not only does your *God* not exist, but you have no place in this College as your very *subject* does not exist! You have no evidence except a clutch of random Aramaic jottings of unknown authorship over 2,000 years ago, *none* of which has been independently verified, let alone subjected to a credible refereeing process! You are dupes of genius – *be gone*'

Uproar.

Order being eventually restored, we moved on to the evolution of Man. Here, thank Heaven (assuming *that* exists), there was at least a degree of consensus. Our Nobel Laureate in Anthropology, the charismatic Aubrey Fitzgerald FRS, gave a riveting account of our remote ancestors slowly trudging out of Africa. Across the Middle East they walked, hunting and gathering pace, before turning north-west and heading in the general direction of Edinburgh.

Behind them, they left our nearest cousin. This is not the gorilla which for all its behavioural similarity to some of my colleagues, is not our closest relative. That honour falls to *Pan paniscus*, the bonobo, an extremely bright variant of *Pan troglodytes*, the chimpanzee. The bonobo is truly remarkable, being apparently more sexually active than the average university undergraduate. The discovery of a new food source will

induce a whole troop of them to engage in a public romp
involving a range of activities only found on the
uppermost shelves magazine shops. When the laughter
had died sufficiently, he went on, 'Their DNA, which my
group has been sequencing,' is no less than 99.2 per cent
identical to ours. In fact we ought to be known
scientifically as *Pan sapiens* – the third Chimp!'

A bonobo called Kanzi, he told the meeting, who lives
in the Primate Learning Sanctuary in Des Moines, Iowa,
can understand 3,000 English words and can articulate
500, though in what order was not clear.

'So bring Kanzi here to give a lecture – or better, chair
a Session!' called a voice from the back.

'Enough!' said I huffily, being currently in the Chair.

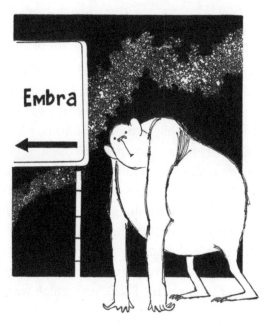

Armistice Day

Office of the Dean

St Andrew's College
King George IV Bridge
Edinburgh EH1 1EE

A SERVICE OF Remembrance was held in Chapel this morning and very moving it was. We had 'I vow to thee my Country' with its tremendous air and first verse and then incomprehensible conclusion. Then prayers. Why the Prebendary *prays* for world peace and reconciliation is beyond me, the evidence from almost all controlled studies being that this activity, however laudable, is totally ineffective.

There was a medical research study some time ago where half of a large group of surgical patients were prayed for, while half weren't. Neither the patients nor the medical and nursing staff in the Infirmary knew who'd had the benefit of an appeal to the Almighty. Only after the patients had been followed up, was the code broken and it could be seen who had got what. The result; those unprayed for did just as well, or badly, as those for whom the Message had gone up.

We had another hymn; 'For those in Peril on the Sea' which took me back to my two years as a new medical graduate on *Canberra*, the P&O liner which was actually a troopship and hospital ship in wartime. Sometimes we would run into a Royal Navy squadron in some foreign port and would all turn out on deck to see and hear 'Sunset'. This is the incredibly moving 'last post' of the Navy played by a Royal Marine bugler and wedded in harmony to 'For those in Peril...' as the White Ensign comes down to close the day.

The solemnity of the Festival of Remembrance last night on TV; the Queen at the Cenotaph this morning; a member of my own family being somewhere tonight in the mountains of Afghanistan, put me in mind of the sheer hardihood of the troops and of their unbreakable, and indispensable, sense of humour.

Some months ago I mentioned the late Peter Ustinov, that peerless *raconteur* that I'd heard at the Saints & Sinners Xmas lunch in London. He described being in a pillbox on the south coast of England in the summer of 1940 waiting, nervously, for the *Wehrmacht*. Private Ustinov was accompanied in the pillbox (a rounded

concrete emplacement with a firing slit) by Private
Goldstein. He was a bespoke Jewish tailor from Warsaw
who'd been caught in London by Hitler's invasion of his
homeland and had been conscripted. Said Ustinov,

'It would be hard to imagine any *less* military pairing
than the two of us, the actor and the tailor... But we
were ready for the Germans. Oh yes. Not only did we
have a rifle, we had *several* rounds of ammunition! But
we also had a major communication problem. Goldstein
had no English, but could speak Polish, Yiddish and
German – while I had Russian, French, German and of
course English.' Thus it came about that the only
language in which these two British Army squaddies
could to talk to each other, was German...

Then came the night of The General Alert; the famous
evening when all units of all Services across the country
were suddenly told:

Invasion expected – and likely within 36 Hours.

Up in Scotland, my late father having finished building
aircraft for the day, was manning a roadblock on the
A77 Glasgow–Ayr road. The barrier was a pyramid of
tree trunks bound together with barbed wire behind
which, shoulder to shoulder, stood a phalanx of peerless
warriors: 'F' Company of the Prestwick Home Guard.
The night was moonless, misty and with the total
blackout, it was as dark as a raven's wing.

Just before midnight, footsteps were heard; far away
down the road at first, but approaching their position.

'Make ready!' hissed the Sergeant in charge. There

was a purposeful rattle of rifle bolts. The footsteps, curiously erratic, still approached.

'Fix bayonets…!' the sounds were closer now – but still nothing visible in the blackness.

'*Halt!*' suddenly bellowed the Sergeant, scaring the daylights out of his men, 'Who – goes – *there*?'

The footsteps stopped dead. Silence. And then from out of the gloom and from not 30 yards away, a Glaswegian voice roared,

'Adolf, f------g, *Hitler!*'

'*FIRE!*'

(They missed him…)

Meanwhile, at about the same time on a Sussex clifftop, the door of the pillbox manned by Messrs. Goldstein & Ustinov opened to admit the Major commanding their unit.

'Cheps,' said he, 'If Jerry lends hyah, as now seems lykleh, the Royal Artillery behind us will 'stonk' this position with a heavy barrage. Consequentleh, our unit has been reclassified and is now a Suicide Battalion. Cleah? Right, keep calm and carry on.' Out he went. Ustinov, now deathly pale, was confronted by an equally alarmed Goldstein who hadn't got a word of the Major's message, but senses that something was very, very wrong –

'Peter, *Peter! Was sagt der Herr Major?*'

Said Ustinov, faintly,

'*Der Herr Major sagt das wir jetzt ein Selbstmord Battalion sind!*' Whereupon Goldstein fainted.

Listening to the great man reminiscing on those times,

it became so clear to us post-war babies listening, that under no circumstances would we, indeed *could* we, lose the war.

The Lord Taverners Lunch

Office of the Dean

St Andrew's College
King George IV Bridge
Edinburgh EH1 1EE

O NE OF THE pleasures of the academic world is
the occasional escape into the parallel Universe
of real life. The so-called ivory tower is actually a
nacreous cocoon in which our intellectual activities are
accompanied by the usual frailties to which human flesh
is heir. Love, hate and envy we have in full measure, but
little gluttony or sloth, presumably since these deadly
sins interfere with the aforesaid hating, envying etc
which drive the academic machine and its operators.

Anyway, today is an escape day. I am to give a speech
at a charitable lunch at an old Edinburgh Club at which
the principal speaker is Christopher Cowdrey. He is the
eldest son of the late Lord Colin, one of the only two
cricketers to be ennobled for their services to the game
and their batting averages for England. Who was the
other, you ask; Learie Constantine of the W. Indies.

Cricket, to the continuing amazement of our English
neighbours, remains an active sport in Scotland. I spent
most of my early years as a child, during which I and my
school friends played the game almost daily in summer,

before succumbing permanently with the golfing bug. The game is old here; in our College archives sits a lithograph of boys playing the game in the schoolyard of the old High School of Edinburgh in 1809, in which year the Peninsular War was still raging in Spain.

At school at Ayr Academy, I was some three years behind that rare bird, a Scottish Captain of England *viz*, MH Denness who would later captain Kent in succession to the aforesaid Colin Cowdrey.

All this reminds me that our Philosophy Department is planning to invite Mike Brearley, another former England Captain, to lecture at College on the nature of captaincy, on which he has written the definitive textbook. After Cambridge, Brearley was a Lecturer in Philosophy at Newcastle University before his cricketing career really took off. As a result he would occasionally discharge his formidable intellect at journalists incautious enough to put questions he considered inconsequential or, worse, tautological. For example, just after his appointment as Captain of the national side, he was ambushed outside Lord's by an Australian reporter. The exchange remains a classic:

Aussie: *Moyke!* Moyke, g'day. Well, hedzit feel ter be Cap'n of England myte?

Brearley: Well, that *very* much depends on what you mean by 'feel' doesn't it? – which in turn is predicated on the sense in which you're deploying that most interesting *concept*, of 'Captain' – which, come to think of it, is also subtended by whether you mean the geographical, the constitutional, or indeed the *intelectual* concept of that fascinating, but admittedly *elusive* entity which, for the purposes of further discussion, we may, may we not, agree to call 'England'.

Aussie: Er... thanks Myke.

But back to today. The charity whose 'Christmas Lunch' is being eccentrically celebrated today in mid-January is The Lord's Taverners. It was founded half a century ago by the actor John Mills and his fellow thespians in the Old Tavern at Lord's cricket ground, home of the Marylebone Cricket Club at St John's Wood in London. Over the years it has raised millions to give kids handicapped in various ways a better start in life – and to encourage youngsters to take up the game.

Lord Colin Cowdrey himself was President some years ago, later succeeded by his eldest son, also a famous wit and orator.

His father delighted in anecdotes of the Duke of Norfolk, the Earl Marshal of England, whose daughter Anne would became Lady Cowdrey. Colin would describe how the Duke faced up to the demon Australian bowler Dennis Lillee when the Aussie touring team played its traditional opening match against the Duke of Norfolk's XI. This was at Arundel, in my view the most beautiful ground in England.

Now, the Australians were under a three-line whip from their management that the Duke, opening the batting with Dennis Amiss of England, was not – repeat *not* – to be dismissed in the first over. However the sight of the premier Pommy Duke taking guard was too much for Lillee. Suffused with ethnic rage, he raced in and sent down an absolute snorter which trapped the old boy absolutely plumb LBW. Up went Lillee, up went the slips and everyone turned to stare at the umpire at the bowler's end – who was the Duke's butler...

Slowly, up went the dreaded finger of doom. Out! The butler then said, as he must have said a hundred times at the Castle door,

'I regret, that His Grace is *not* in...'

The Duke was a great character. In his capacity as Earl Marshal of England, equivalent to the Duke of Hamilton in Scotland, he superintended such State Events as the funeral of Sir Winston Churchill. I was at a dinner once where he outlined the exigencies of his exalted position, saying that he had been in his Estate Office in Norfolk when the telephone rang.

All the staff had popped out at that moment, so one was there alone and faced with a dilemma; should one ignore it, which seemed discourteous; or should one answer it? But answering it meant another dilemma; what on earth should one *say*? Should one say 'Earl Marshal of England here', which sounded rather heavy, or 'Bernard Fitzalan-Howard here', which sounded rather too matey. So I decided to simply tell the truth. I picked it up and I said into it, 'Duke of Norfolk here!' Immediately, I heard a hand go down over the receiver at the other end as a voice shouted, 'Mabel, *wot* were that number? I'm speaking to a *Pub*!'

And so, leaving Academia to its own devices for an hour or so – I'm off to bat, bowl and field with the Taverners.

Student Japes

Office of the Dean

St Andrew's College
King George IV Bridge
Edinburgh EH1 1EE

D ESPITE HAVING no students ourselves at St Andrew's, the President expects us to contribute to under-graduate education elsewhere in various ways such as lecturing and invigilating over at the University. Invigilation means wearing a black gown and a severe expression while walking up and down the aisles quaking inwardly at the difficulty of the exam paper. However, it otherwise just involves dozing in a chair at the front of the vast Founder's Hall while the examinees, known as 'candidates', scribble away; or reading *Trainspotting* concealed behind *The Times Higher Education Supplement*. However this year, there was an interruption...

Towards the end of Whitsun Term I was invigilating the Classical Greek finals with the learned and appropriately named Dr Hector MacDonald. It was a warm Edinburgh afternoon; flies occasionally buzzed, sunbeams slanted through the high windows, high-lighting motes in the still air. All was peace and rustling concentration as the students wrote for their lives.

Then, without warning, the outer door opened. In

came a student wearing a waiter's white jacket and carrying a tray upon which was a pint glass beside a canister of Baird's Special Export Ale. He marched down an aisle past the hunched candidates and placed the tray on the table of a candidate, later found to be his flat mate. He then attempted to leave. He did not get far; Hector collared him.

'Stop! Just what are you about, creature?' demanded he.

In response, the 'waiter' pulled out from his jacket what proved to a copy of an *Ordynance* of the University, dated MDLXV (1565). With the Latin title '*De Cibis Vinisque Discipulorum*' this remarkable edict decreed in rich mediaeval Scots, that during written examinations, undergraduates might be 'slockened wyth ale', i.e. have their thirst quenched with a brew. A hurried call to my friend Bertie Wood, the University's archivist, confirmed the waiter's stout claim that this *Ordynance* had never been rescinded. It was still in force…

Hector and I looked at each other in alarm; for we knew what might now happen. It did.

Five more times during the examination, the door opened. Five more times a canister of Baird's best was placed before the increasingly slockened candidate – and five more times the smirking waiter swept out past us, the *Ordynance* sticking cheekily out of his white jacket.

Next morning, the recipient of the ale appeared before the formidable Prof. Charles Ramsay-Gardiner, Dean of Classics. The exchange was appropriately classic:

CR-G: I am aware of yesterday's performance.

Student: Good, sir.

CR-G: *Not* good, sirrah! Do you *really* believe that an Ordinance of 1565 should retain today the relevance it possessed at the time of its promulgation half a *millennium* ago?'

Student: I do indeed.

CR-G: So do I. Now, here is another *Ordynance*, this one dated MDLIX which imposes a fine of 50 Merks for *not* wearing a sword... Furthermore, since you advocate strongly that Ordynances retain their original force, let me tell you that today 50 Merks amounts to some £75.50. Pay the Bursar. Now, *Out!*

There is an interesting term in the '*Ordynance*' quoted above. The old Scots verb to *slocken* means to assuage thirst. According to Angus Og MacLeod of Bragar, our Professor of Scots Literature, it probably has the same etymological root as *slake* in English.

It can also mean to *quench*, at least it did to Lord Buccleuch in the famous *Ballad of Kinmont Willie*, published by Sir Walter Scott in his *Minstrelsy*. The eponymous hero Willie Armstrong of Kinmont was a classic ruffian and an expert in the mediaeval Borders specialties of theft, assault, arson and culpable homicide. He was also a notorious 'reiver', a person deeply committed to the cross-border livestock transportation industry.

Caught red-handed with 300 English cattle by Lord Thomas Scrope, Warden of the West March, Willie of

Kinmont had been banged up, or rather banged down, into the dungeons of Carlisle Castle. He had been also promised a 'fair' trial, i.e. one with a fair expectation of the gallows.

Back in Scotland, his feudal boss was Lord Walter Scott of Buccleuch. Known as '*The Bauld*' (bold, not bald) Buccleuch, he was incensed at the loss not only of a top reiver, but also of the hundreds of rump steaks Willie had been escorting back to Drumlanrig Castle. He burst out with a great blast of Scots, the old language redolent as always with graphic imagery and verbal firepower:

I will set Carlisle Castell in ane Lowe!   [conflagration]
And slockene it wyth Englyshe Blude!   [douse, quench]
Till there is nae man in Cumberland
Shall ken whaur Carlisle Castell stude!   [know]

Buccleuch then mounted one of the classic commando raids of our history. He entered England with an elite squad of cross-border livestock transport executives, forded the Eden, scaled the walls of Carlisle Castle, sprang Kinmont Willie from durance vile – and back to Scotland.

Queen Elizabeth I was not amused.

Those were the days, my friend, we thought they'd never end... but they did, thanks to the Union.

A Summer Roundup

Office of the Dean

St Andrew's College
King George IV Bridge
Edinburgh EH1 1EE

HIGH SUMMER IN Edinburgh and it's wet – *very* wet. The Jetstream (about which the Government seems utterly powerless) normally sweeps in over the Shetlands bringing anticyclones and fine weather, but not this year. It's been abducted south by the perfidious French. The thing now sweeps in over Bordeaux, bringing a stratospheric conveyer-belt of Atlantic depressions with a daily dumping of downpours on us. Fed up with this, I consulted our tropospherologist Dr Hirohito Takayatsu as to what might be done: 'Buy new umblerra; world weather machine totarry *chaotic!*'

I reminded him that his own weather machine, a supercomputer ominously called BORIS and capable of 3.4 trillion calculations per second, had been bought for him by the College at vast expense. (Also vast is its electrical consumption; when they switch it on, the lights dim in the Holyrood parliament)

'Hiro,' said I, 'surely Chaos Theory could resolve this. Consult BORIS.'

Two weeks and innumerable calculations later, the

answer came. It was astonishing. Just as the *El Niño* phenomenon in the Pacific had been due to a butterfly flapping about in Madagascar – so Takayatsu found that the wettest Edinburgh summer for a century was apparently caused by an ape overbalancing and falling out of a tree in the Congo. I may yet believe this.

Our Bedellus, Mr McEachran and our Clerk of Works (appropriately named Mr Clarke), accompany me each summer on the traditional 'vacation rounds' where we inspect the rooms and suites of the absent Dons and Fellows. I never cease to marvel at what we discover to be the extra-curricular interests of some of the brightest minds in the country.

For example, a scrabbling noise in Dr Ragworth's wardrobe proved to be an enraged *Mustela putorius* (common ferret) wearing a collar inscribed, curiously, 'Property of Stockbridge Golf Club.' Our entry to Prof. von Schlacht's suite was delayed by the usual booby-trap; this time a spring-loaded launcher, complete with deceased pigeon, while in the study of Prof. Mackendrick (Theology) was a complete set of a 'Journal' whereof it is unlawful to speak. In general, however, we found that the old place seems to be in a reasonable degree of structural health.

Speaking of degrees, I had a most disagreeable note this week from our President rejecting my proposal of an LLD (*honoris causa*) for Henry McMerrie on the grounds

that he (McMerrie) is dead. I see no reason why this engineering genius and father of EDMET, the new and long overdue Edinburgh Metro, should not be honoured, albeit *post-mortem*.

The reason, I bet, was a noisy and fume-laden Metro airshaft. This object broke surface recently in the President's private garden, depositing a layer of sooty hydrocarbons on his perennials.

I should say that even by Nobel Laureate standards (his Prize was in Physics) the President is distinctly odd. After five minutes in conversation with him, I find myself saying,

'Is it him – or is it me...?'

His residence and garden is known privately to the Dons as the 'TZ' – for Twilight Zone. The name comes from the classic US televisual series, each episode of which began with Rod Sterling's sonorous baritone welcoming viewers to the fifth dimension, the Twilight Zone...

He was right; there *is* such a place and it's right here! In the Presidential TZ, relativity rules as the quantum reality of the Multiverse begins. Entering it, one senses the Uncertainty Principle of Heisenberg while peering around nervously for Schrödinger's cat. Only the Metro flue spouts reality.

And so, poor Harry McMerrie's Hon. LLD has been literally air-shafted. His ghost will have to haunt the EDMET tunnels and, in Wilfred Owens' phrase, 'up the flues make moan', alas for evermore.

The Royal garden party at the Palace of Holyroodhouse

this week was its usual wondrous self, but the best came last.

During the clearing up, inside a large bush, there was found a complete set of NHS false teeth firmly embedded in a Holyrood toffee bun. Some edentulous country Provost must have sunk them into the confection, only to find their withdrawal a different matter as the Royal party approached...

One can only imagine the subsequent exchange with the Queen's consort:

D of E: Come far?

Provost: MMmm... mmm

D of E: Excellent. Here with a partner?

Provost: Mmmamma...

D of E: Really? She must be a good age by now...

The AGM

Office of the Dean

St Andrew's College
King George IV Bridge
Edinburgh EH1 1EE

THE APPROACH of the Annual General Meeting of this
College in Whitsun Term is a time of unparalleled
tension for the Dean, Bursar, Prebendary, Bedellus and
indeed all members of the *Estaitis*, our ancient Scots
word for a Council. The President, Lord Fanshawe
FRS, CH, OM presides. We all sit like Aunt Sallies on
the platform of Great Hall in front of an audience of
all the Dons and Fellows, the external assessors, Town
Councillors, the Minister for Higher Education (in
person) and, to cap it all the prowling jackals of both the
academic and the gutter press.

The procedure is relatively unchanged from our
Foundation in 1561 when the then *Privy Counsell* of
Scotland and the *Tounis Counsell* of Edinburgh laid
down the format. They also laid down that, '*In alle Tyme
comyng*', the AGM would be a public meeting, so there's
no escape. Interestingly, for over two centuries the
occasion used to begin with a reading of 'Ye Riot Acte'
(1543) which suggests that proceedings were, to say the
least, lively. They still are...

Starting with an interminable 'Prayer for Divine Intercession' by the prebendary, we than proceed to the presidential homily (curiously on lobster-cloning this time) followed by the Bursar who's always commendably brief. Said he,

'My Lord President, colleagues, ladies and gentlemen, I am pleased to announce that, for the 156th year in succession, College *income* has exceeded *expenditure*. Are there *any* questions? No? Right. Next item of Business...'

And then it's my turn to give the Academic Review of the year. This encompasses our research activity, our output of books, chapters, papers in refereed journals etc, all frightfully boring, and our prizes. Sadly, no Nobel

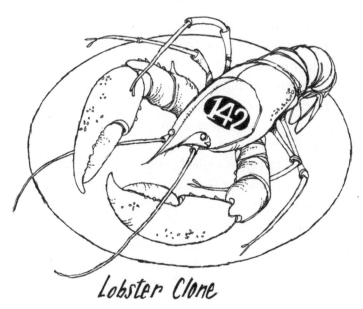

Lobster Clone

laureate this year. The Physics Prize for which Prof. Smailholm and his team were shortlisted in Stockholm, was probably lost through the damage suffered by the Anti-Gravity Lab and indeed the entire building, in the tremendous explosion consequent on their attempts to create a Black Hole.

Mind you, as I told the AGM, things were just as violent in 1651 after the Civil War in which many of the Covenanters among the Dons had taken part on the Parliamentary side, with their Royalist colleagues on the other. In order to conclude my remarks on a lighter note, I read to the meeting the Report of the AGM of that year.

College yf Sanct Andrewes

Know ye All & Sundry that; Ane plenary Meetyng of the said College, convened ye 14th daye of July in the yeare of Grace MDCLVI. Amen.

The Deane bade courteous welcome unto the Preses & Fellows & the Lord Provost of Edynburghe & sundrie persouns.

Dean & Faculty stoode uncovered in pyous Memory of Fellows killed in the late Civil Warre & in remembrance of Hys Majestie King Charles I, an Hon. Fellow of College, lately beheaded before hys Palace of Whitehall.

The Treasurer & Remembrancer, being called, gave no true account of the Accounts, onlye crying with great boldnesse that Expenditure had exceeded Income & straightway drew hys sworde saying, 'Was there any Question?

Whereupon Sir Thos. Brodie rose & called hym ane thiefe, a varlet & a villein & drew hys sword & closed with hym, whereupon the Deane, crying Order, Order! drew & fyred his pistole in the aire which severed the corde causing the candelabrum to fall upon Dr Mackenzie-Stuart, Jas. Haswell Esq., the Minister of St Giles & divers others to their injury who, being incensed, the combatte became generall, & errupted outwith the College into the streete & there contynued until the Lord Provoste, causing the City Guard to dyscharge a volley over their heddes, brought order.

All being returned into College, the Deane earnestlie desired Members to refraine from vyolence, mindful that some were but lately combatant in the hatefulle Civil Warre & were unused to peece.

Dr Richard Pyke Esq., then rose & asked by what right was Lord Wedderburn & hys sultrie mistresse suffered to lurch around the College park & grounds in his Carriage & Four, followed by hys pack of houndes ? For the ruttes caused by hys L'dship's carriage wheeles & the droppyngs of hys horses & dogges were a damn'd nuisance. Wherefore he moved that Ld. Wedderburn be censured therewith.

Thereupon Ld. Wedderburn rose & called Pyke

for a damned Roundhedde and turned hys back upon hym – whereat Dr Pyke did say,

I be not affronted, Gentlemen, for verily I have seene hys Back before! Aye, 'twas at the battle of Marston Moore, wherefrom he did runne away & at great speede!

Whereat Ld. Wedderburn swoare a great oathe & said he did not runne away – but was onlye retreating! He called Pyke for a Kern & a Gallowglass – how dare he speake thus to mee, a Peer of the Realme of ancyent lineage back to blessed King Canmore's tyme – mee, a nobleman flyted by a wastrel who cannot trace hys ancestrie back to hys father!

There being no other Busyness, the Deane called Halte! & desired that all would proceed unto Greate Halle to dyne in peece and harmonie.

Attestit, Sygnit & Sealit by me,
Edward Douglas, Esquire; Hon. Coll. Secretar.

Gravity

Office of the Dean

St Andrew's College
King George IV Bridge
Edinburgh EH1 1EE

A FAMOUS REDE lecture was given half a century ago in the Senate House at Cambridge, by CP Snow. In it, he advocated that the two sides of the academic Quadrangle, i.e. the Sciences and the Humanities, should not just be just dimly aware of each other's existence and subject-matter. They should actually *talk* to each other. This can be difficult...

I was trained in the Sciences, but now research in the literature and philosophy of the 18th century. I thus have a foot in both camps, but it's not easy. Oh for the days of the original Oyster Club founded by David Hume, Adam Smith, James Hutton and other superstars of the Enlightenment, when the entirety of human knowledge was within the grasp of polymaths such as these. In the 21st century we're all highly specialised with our own vocabularies and terms of reference. Thus for a philosopher to get a handle, let alone a grip, on what a physiologist is talking about – and vice versa, is a serious trial.

However, one should make the effort. With that in mind, this week I attended a meeting of the staff of our AGL (Anti-Gravity Lab) to try, yet again, to understand what gravity actually *is*. This is *not* easy. I remember hearing that Einstein, lecturing at the Institute for Advanced Study at Princeton, was wandering about as usual and waving his pipe while saying to the class in his classical German accent:

'Und zo, I pose the kvestion vonce mohr. Vot *iss* zis force, zis enigma. *Vot iss Gravity?*'

Now, he meant the question to be rhetorical, no answer then being possible. But to his surprise, a student put his hand up.

'Yes?' said the great man quizzically to the student who immediately began to look uncomfortable,

'I'm *so* sorry, Professor Einstein' he said. 'It *was* there, but now, I'm afraid... No, it's gone.'

'Oh *no!*' cried the sage, 'the *only* man in the Universe who *knew* vot voss Gravity – und he's forgotten!'

It seems that now we do know. Gravity is a bending of the Higgs field. He of the famously elusive Boson, also gave his name to an invisible field which exists, well, everywhere. We can't see it, touch it or even visualise it, but it's right here, there, and everywhere. And it can be bent. All objects with mass, defined as a body's ability to have inertia, bend it.

My keyboard here bends it, you yourself bend it, the Earth bends it. The bigger the mass, the tighter the bend and the stronger the pull towards the centre of that mass.

Another extraordinary aspect of gravity is how *weak* its force actually is. It may seem strong enough to us, but consider this. The gravitational pull of the *entire earth* is insufficient to stop you or me jumping, i.e. leaving the ground! Indeed Olympic athletes can jump nearly three *metres* off the planet, before falling back to Earth. We're also designed for it and evolved in it. The human body's architecture is precisely adapted to Earth's gravity. Take away that gravity and we do badly.

I was once in Houston at the Johnson Spaceflight Centre to discuss osteoporosis, normally a malady of the elderly, but also a major problem for Astronauts. If you're weightless for any length of time, your muscles get flabby and stop doing their job; essentially to act as levers pulling on your bones. The bones themselves sense this lack of muscle pull, reacting by shedding calcium and ultimately, strength.

Thus the NASA Mars Mission, which my colleagues and I were briefed on, was in trouble. It's nine months to Mars and nine months back. If the astronaut trips on the ladder on exiting the Lander and falls to Earth – correction, Mars – and breaks a leg, well there's no A&E or orthopaedic help around the corner.

The answer is to simulate gravity by spinning the crew quarters on the Marsliner en route to the red planet, at a speed of rotation whose centrifugal force will mimic Earth's gravity. I think they did this in Kubrick's film *2001: A Space Odyssey* – to music by Strauss.

So, mass is conferred on everything by the Higgs

Boson. Its work done, it vanishes in a trillionth of a second, decaying into a stream of baryons, whatever *they* are. Gravity is conferred by the Higgs field and a lot of my College's money is poured into our AGL here in the hope of reversing it – or 'ploughing up the Higgs field' as the inmates call it.

They are a remarkable and dangerous bunch, particularly when experimenting with antimatter...

I should point out that the collision of matter with antimatter is to be avoided. Each annihilates the other with a violence, as A. Einstein predicted, of Energy = mc^2. When one reflects that 'c' is the speed of light and measures 300,000 km/sec, you can see why I appealed to them to be careful. They were trying to figure out what gravitation pull is exerted by a lump of matter, known for some reason as a 'sausage' – on a lump of antimatter known, predictably, as an anti-sausage. They found that the pull of one on the other was increasing exponentially as the sausages approached each other, so the two were further approximated until they were only a few femtometres (10^{-15} metres) apart. At that precise moment, someone pulled the chain in the staff toilet next door. The slunge from the cistern shook the lab just a few picometres but it was enough. Sausage and anti-sausage united...

The resulting explosion brought down the roof, blew out every window in the streets outside and measured 4.9 on the Richter Scale downstairs in the Geophysics lab. It measured fully 10.0 on our College President's own Richter scale, when he saw the bill for the repairs, especially as he was still grumping about the AGL's last debacle. This was when when their huge (15 Tesla) magnetic field escaped into the street outside, magnetizing every passing metal object including a garbage truck and a City Council's surveillance drone.

In short, I had a tough time explaining to him that the latest blast was, yet again, for the greater good of Science.

He'll get over it, I trust.

Founder's Day Lecture

Office of the Dean

St Andrew's College
King George IV Bridge
Edinburgh EH1 1EE

THERE WAS A dramatic conclusion last night to the annual Founder's Lecture which I have to chair in the Great Hall. This year it was given by the Nobel laureate economist Aidan Hartigan of All Souls, Oxford. The event had taken its usual course before a capacity audience, the lecture title being 'The Role of Complex Variables in the Public Sector Borrowing Requirement'.

This, I was assured by our own economists, was an electrifying subject. I could only weakly agree, the very thought of 60 minutes on the PSBR filling one with utter dread. Anyway, after a full hour of incomprehensible economic technobabble, accompanied by projected images of total obscurity, it came mercifully to an end.

Then came the Q&A session which I chaired. This brought our guest into direct confrontation with Prof. Harry Mackenzie from Glasgow University whose model of the UK economy is apparently at loggerheads with Hartigan's. Indeed, the pair of them had squared off recently in the columns of *Macroeconomics Today*, a publication with which I am thankfully unfamiliar.

I had been warned to keep them apart, since a collision would resemble the matter/antimatter explosion here which blew out half the windows in this part of Edinburgh. However, before I could stop him, MacKenzie jumped up and accused our guest of denying that in the conventional Keynesian use of the AS–AD model, the aggregate supply curve is horizontal at low levels of output and may even become 'inelastic'. This was totally beyond me, but is apparently the economic equivalent of high treason. The response was dramatic. Hartigan went puce in the face, made as if to speak and then to our amazement hurled himself forwards from the podium. He literally flew into Mackenzie knocking him off his seat in a magnificent rugby tackle. Chaos ensued. I pulled them apart and hustled Hartigan into the anteroom while a badly shaken Mackenzie was hauled off to the SCR for a stiffener.

'Was the question *that* offensive?' I asked.

'It wasn't the question,' gasped Hartigan. 'It was the PAS!'

'The what?'

'Progressive Anorectal Stenosis. Type II.'

'I *see...*' said I, seeing only fog.

However, having heard him out and checked with our College physicians, I see now.

Aidan Hartigan's problem is of great rarity, yet of fascination to the general public. It flares up episodically and without warning, causing its victims total embarrassment and sometimes injury. Like its neurological cousin

the Gilles de la Tourette syndrome, it is autonomous and capricious. However, unlike Tourette's, the problem was not up in the head. It is down, well down, below…
Aidan indeed has Progressive Anorectal Stenosis (PAS), also known as de Laval Syndrome after the Swedish scientist whose nozzle principle it illustrates.

As its name implies, PAS is a condition of the rectum or terminal bowel. For reasons still obscure, this becomes progressively narrowed or *stenosed*, leading to a spectacular increase in the speed of gases passing along it. In most cases, classed as PAS Type I, this is not a major issue since it can be detected by barium studies and corrected surgically.

However, in the rarer but much more serious PAS Type II, as in Hartigan's case, the rectal narrowing is exacerbated by bowel spasms induced by the gas hydrogen sulphide (H2S). These spasms narrow the rectum even further, thus accelerating the already fast-passing gas, or wind, to extreme velocities.

In these circumstances, it can be clearly seen that the emergent velocity (Ve) of gas leaving the rectum will be given by the equation:

$$V_e = \sqrt{\frac{T\,R}{M} \cdot \frac{2\,k}{k-1} \cdot \left[1 - (P_e/P)^{(k-1)/k}\right]}$$

The actual Ve of escaping wind can reach up to 150 mph and effectively turns the terminal bowel into what is known in aviation as a ramjet. A colicky spasm is the only warning the patient receives that the anorectal ramjet is about to fire. He knows then to hold on tight to any available structure, since he is about to be powerfully subjected to Newton's Third Law of Motion. Depending on the direction in which his rear is pointing when the ramjet ignites, the patient is instantly propelled up to eight feet forwards, if standing, or one foot upwards if recumbent. The volume of expelled gas being relatively small, the episode is not malodorous, while the noise it creates – a thin, high pitched scream – is usually drowned by the even higher-pitched yell of the subject and the equally alarmed cries of those toward whom he is being projected.

Not surprisingly, those afflicted by PAS Type II take precautions such as avoiding dietary items that generate colonic hydrogen sulphide. In former times this was not possible and indeed Dr Marcus Ralston of this College has speculated that the disorder may finally explain certain odd incidents in recorded history. Since high emotion provokes bowel activity, he postulates that if a person with PAS Type II were to find himself acutely frightened while carrying a load of colonic H_2S, the results could literally, be explosive. For example, in the 9th century, there was the remarkable behaviour of King Egfrith of Northumbria. While sailing in his personal galley off Jarrow, a large Viking fleet was sighted approaching. What happened next is described thus in Latin by the chronicler Oswiulf of York:

> tandem in puppem regem adligavere quia in mare seriatim propulsus erat.

'Eventually they lashed the King to the poop, since he had repeatedly hurled himself into the sea.'

Scholars puzzled over this passage for centuries. No longer! While a fast-approaching Viking squadron would give anyone a degree of intestinal anxiety, it would seem that on this occasion PAS Type II, compounded by H2S, perhaps from some dodgy eggs, had given Egfrith a series of right royal ramjets. (He would get another, courtesy of Erik 'Bloodaxe' Sigurdsson, later in the day...)

Now, you can probably see where this is leading. Aidan Hartigan explained the great care he takes with both his diet and his bodily positioning, in order to minimise an attack. He always stands more than eight feet back from any precipice and descends staircases backwards, while keeping pace with those descending conventionally.

In bed he wears a crash helmet (as does Mrs Hartigan) and he sleeps prone rather than supine, the bedstead reinforced by multiple cushions nailed to the headboard. Nevertheless there are occasional disasters.

A keen golfer, he was spectating at the Open Championship at St Andrews last year when a spasm sent him jetting into the leader, Juan Gonzalez of Spain, who was about to take a rather important putt. Ordered by R&A officials to leave the course and restrict himself to the tented village, he headed straight for the Bollinger Tent.

'It was really no hardship at all,' he told me, 'because there's yet another advantage to champagne.'

'So what's that?' said I.

'It puts out the pilot-light on the gas!'

Appraisals

Office of the Dean

St Andrew's College
King George IV Bridge
Edinburgh EH1 1EE

CANDLEMAS TERM and it's appraisal time for our Research Fellows; and nowadays that means days of non-stop box ticking. Gone are the days when the Dean would simply call them in, one by one, review their activities, look over their papers published in learned Journals – and then give them their 'Traffic Light':

Green for Go;

Amber for Admonition;

Red for Rustication (i.e. out!)

Of course the process was subjective. But I and my predecessors knew from dealing with them day-to-day how well they were doing, or otherwise. It was quick and it worked; well, usually.

Then in the 1980s with what Shakespeare calls a flourish of trumpets, enter the Administrators! A Fellow now can't be assessed without showing not only his/her research publications, but also the 'Impact Factor' of each article. This nefarious process produces a 'Score' from 1–10 based not only on the 'prestige' of the journal carrying the piece, but also on the number of times the article has been cited by researchers in other journals, again scored on *their* prestige – whatever that is.

In other words, a major paper in *Nature* or *Science* or *The Lancet* is likely to score 10, whereas God help you if it's buried somewhere in the *Hibernian Journal of Comparative Ontology*.

Most papers, chapters, books and encyclopedias emanating from this College do get cited all over the place, but there are casualties. I had a tearful Dr Ramsay Wedderburn in the Deanery this morning, mortified that his *Magnum Opus* had not been cited, or reviewed, anywhere.

Admittedly his book, *British Army Laundry Services in the Ashanti Campaign, 1873–4* was never going to race up *The Times* Best Seller list. However, as Wedderburn pointed out (at great length) the entire

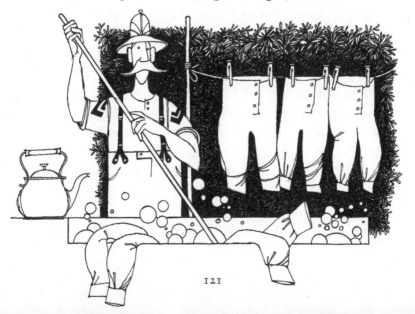

campaign would have been lost had the dreaded *Dhobi-Itch* which had immobilised whole battalions, not been overcome by mandatory pantaloon boiling. One can see the force both of this argument – and indeed of the Dhobi-Itch, the very mention of which makes me want to go. Alas, Wedderburn's tome, like David Hume's *Treatise of Human Nature* had, in Hume's own memorable phrase, 'fallen dead-born from the press'.

I comforted the crushed Wedderburn. I told him that Hume's work did not die; indeed it would rise again, becoming the manifesto of the Enlightenment itself – just as his *Ashanti Campaign* would become the manifesto of military laundry services everywhere. Curiously, he seemed comforted by this.

The Appraisal process takes many forms and is fraught with danger. In particular, the writing of Assessments which are critical of someone's research work, or indeed character, has to be done with care. It's not easy to say bluntly that a bonehead is a bonehead without causing offence and, as in several recent cases, a legal action for slander.

The way around this minefield is to damn with praise so faint as to require a microscope to see it: e.g., 'This PhD student, on the few occasions I have been able to find him, seems a fairly reasonable sort of chap...'

The alternative, brought out only occasionally and handled with extreme care, is that fearful, camouflaged weapon – *irony*!

'This Lecturer has, from the moment of his arrival at

St Andrew's College, performed his many and exacting duties *entirely* to his own satisfaction.'

Things were so much easier for our forefathers with their pithy one-liner references; and the masters of this were Army Colonels in their Annual Reports on young officers:

'I would not *breed* from this Officer.'

'This Officer is depriving some rural village of an *Idiot*.'

'The men will follow this Officer *anywhere*; not from loyalty, but from a tremendous sense of curiosity…'

The Royal Navy was not far behind:

'This Midshipman is using my Frigate to carry his genitals from port to port; but not from port to starboard.'

'Lieutenant X has delusions of adequacy, compounded from the experience of extreme youth allied to the enthusiasm of terminal old age. He should go far – and the sooner the better.'

My own former medical colleagues, particularly those blunt, i.e. extremely sharp, Consultant Surgeons of the Royal Infirmary were adept in the art of the tart reference. There was a famous one from Sir Lancelot Scott, FRCS, (memorably portrayed as 'Spratt' on screen by James Robertson Justice).

Dear Sir;
        Re: Dr R------- C--------
Daniel: Chap. V; Verse XXVII.
    Yours sincerely,
            Scott

A copy of the Good Book was eventually found, opened and *Daniel* examined. Verse 27 of Chapter 5 runs:

> Behold, he is weighed in the Balances – and found wanting...

Whole academic disciplines sometimes get a blistering reference. For example, Philosophy is one of the dominant disciplines here at St Andrew's College and one of prestige events is our annual Bertrand Russell Memorial Lecture. As I reported last week, this year's 'Bertie' was delivered by Prof. Lionel Trelawney of Cambridge, before his adventure with our stairlift and the laundry chute.

The Lord Russell Lecture always reminds me of the London cabbie taking me to University College, London to give a lecture. He told me he'd once had 'that Bertrand Russell', the celebrated philosopher in the back. Stuck at the lights between the House of Lords and the Athenaeum, the cabbie looked up at his mirror and asked, unwittingly, the central question in all philosophy:

Cabbie: Ok then Lawd Russell, wossit all abaht then?

Russell: I beg your pardon?

Cabbie: This life, yer Lawdship. Wossit all *abaht*?

Russell: (reflective pause) Actually, we have *no* idea...

'So there yer are, Guv,' says the cabbie at Gower St as I paid him off at UCL's front door. 'Flosophy? *Tow'al* wysta toyme!

Trains

Office of the Dean

St Andrew's College
King George IV Bridge
Edinburgh EH1 1EE

I HAVE RECENTLY returned to College from a most agreeable foray into England to give a lecture in the equally agreeable City of Liverpool. Home of a great university, Liverpool also boasts the Walker Art Gallery with its sensational collection of paintings by Sir Laurence Alma-Tadema the pre-eminent interpreter of scenes from classical Greece and Rome. However, I was not there to gaze at Caesar Augustus or the Nymphs of Baiae, delectable as the latter are. I was there to talk about James Boswell, our great biographer and the man who broke the hagiographic mould of the genre – literally inventing the modern pen-picture in book form. But more of JB anon.

My travelling was by train since I now always take to the rails when a service is available. Sir Richard Branson, whom may the Gods preserve, has instituted an excellent service from Edinburgh to Birmingham New Street station, calling *inter alia* at Lockerbie, Carlisle and Preston. There I alighted to be met by my host for the drive to Liverpool.

The whole process was interesting and instructive. It began with my presenting myself to the First Class waiting room of Edinburgh's Waverley station, only to be thrown out! It transpired that the ticket I held was of the inferior '1st Class Advance' species, which denied advancement into the said waiting room. Interesting. 'Book *early!*' cry the ads; omitting to say that such prescience means ejection from a comfortable wait.

Right; off I went to freeze quietly on the concourse until, bang on time, in sighed *The Pendolino*, a tilting train of eight carriages attended by a numerous and courteous staff. The tilt is noticeable when the assemblage negotiates a curve – which it does in the manner of a motorcycle or an aeroplane by 'banking' to left or right, while maintaining a steady 120 mph. I have always calculated train speeds since my father showed me the quarter-mile trackside markers as we sped past in those far-off days of steam. Half a century later the markers are still there, but power is now supplied by Dr Rudolf Diesel. *The Pendolino* took exactly 7.5 seconds to pass from one quarter-mile marker to the next; hence it was doing one mile in 30 seconds – or 120mph.

Several improvements might be made to rail journeys with little extra expense. For example, a serious 'whiplash' neck injury might be sustained as the train rockets through a non-stop station and one flicks one's head desperately from right to left in order to read its name. By my calculations, the last sign at either end of the main platform, if angled at 17.5 degrees away from the track, would allow passengers to slow down their neck-flicks to below the whiplash threshold. I shall write to Sir Richard about this.

Another problem is the existential nature of the onboard announcements. At the end of my journey home, the PA system declared, alarmingly,

'At the station approaching, Edinburgh Waverley, this *train* will terminate,' i.e. technically, cease to *exist*. The intention clearly was that the *service* would terminate, but for any veteran of St Andrew's College Philosophy seminars, the effect was frankly terrifying. Given that Waverley is itself a Terminus, the message might be adjusted to: 'Next stop, Waverley *Terminus*!'

There were also repeated appeals by the PA system for departing passengers to *please* ensure that they take *all* luggage and personal belongings with them. Personal belongings, note, not necessarily their own…

However, *much* more contentious was the *first* part of nearly all announcements from the Customer Services Supervisor (the guard); to the effect that '*the station approaching is…*' There followed the name: Carlisle, Oxenholme, Lancaster, etc. Now, is this correct? Is the station indeed approaching the *train* – or, is the train approaching the *station*? Back at College, discussions with our astrophysicists and theoretical quantum dynamicists resulted in an interesting consensus. In terms of the nine-dimensional Einsteinian space-time continuum, the station *was* actually approaching the train. The guard was correct! I thus commend the spatio-temporal precision of train crews, as their splendid *Pendolinos* warp smoothly and *relatively* across the British cosmos.

As the train pulled into Carlisle on the way home, I immediately thought of Alexander McCall Smith and his latest book in the 44 *Scotland Street* series. This one is called *Bertie's Guide to Life & Mothers* – and I am in it. Bertie (aged seven) is the precocious, Spanish-speaking, saxophone-playing, Steiner School-educated, victim of a ferociously ambitious mother. In the course of a walk in Edinburgh's New Town with his dad Stuart Pollock, Bertie is taken (Chapter 32) past my ancient private residence and is told by Stuart about my Carlisle Story. This, I reckon to be one of the classics of Anglo-Scottish relations and of the West Coast mainline that unites us.

An English company director has just boarded the Night Sleeper at Euston for a business trip to Glasgow when he gets a text-message from his Chairman. Trouble has broken out in the firm's Carlisle factory and he is to break his journey north at Carlisle and sort this out.

He approaches the Aberdonian sleeping-car attendant with the necessity of alighting at Carlisle, but is told that the train only halts momentarily there at 5 in the morning for a driver change. It is *not* a 'Station Stop'.

However, £50 quietly changes hands and it's a deal. He'll be awakened on the approach and hustled out on Carlisle Station at 5a.m.

Excellent. He goes to sleep north of London – and wakes up in daylight. He rushes to the window. The

train is slowly approaching Glasgow Central. Carlisle is
120 miles back down the line… he gets dressed and in a
towering rage he goes out, finds and corners the
attendant, giving him *both* barrels at point-blank range
in expletive-undeleted language.

Eventually, all passion spent, he throws out his bags
and stamps off the train; whereupon the attendant leans
on the open window, saying,

'I'm awfy sorry; my fault entirely. Nae excuses. But
I'll say this for you, Sir. Ye're a *grand* swearer. Tremendous!

Ye're *almost* as good as him we *did* put oot at
Carlisle.'

The Dean from Krakow

Office of the Dean

St Andrew's College
King George IV Bridge
Edinburgh EH1 1EE

THE FESTIVAL AND its raucous Fringe roars on. I had a pleasant Fringe duty this year at the Book Festival. This event occupies the entire central area of Edinburgh's Charlotte Square and is attended by thousands. They came, as Burns says, from 'a' the airts', i.e. every compass direction to buy books, attend signings by authors or to listen to them being interviewed in the Main Marquee. This structure seats *c.*800 and here I was to read aloud at one of the events therein.

Each year, my friend Alexander McCall Smith is interviewed onstage in the Marquee, often by Jim Naughtie of the BBC's *Today* programme. The event sells out in minutes and the whole affair is sponsored by Bonham's the great auction house. Before a packed house, Sandy discusses his latest book which may be of the *44 Scotland Street* series, or an *Isabel Dalhousie* detective work, or whatever has taken his pen recently. Writing with fluency and dry wit at an astonishing 1,000 words per hour, the output streams from him. This is a rate of composition far beyond the capacity or the

competency of such as your humble servant, who is pleased with 1,000 words per *day*. Indeed, should he ever ask me if I've read all his books, I'll have the truthful answer ready;

'No! You write faster than I can read...'

Anyway, this year I had to read a chapter from one of the latest in the *44 Scotland Street* series: viz *Bertie's Guide to Life & Mothers*. The latter is Irene Pollock, the ultimate in pushy Edinburgh New Town matrons whose child Bertie (*aetatis suae* VII) is being groomed, if not for the House of Commons, then certainly for the Bench, or the Bridge of an aircraft-carrier of the superior sort. Bertie attends the Steiner School in Edinburgh, speaks Italian and undergoes, reluctantly, psychoanalysis by a shrink who is loosely based on the father of the (sadly late) Nicky Fairbairn QC, Solicitor General of Scotland and one of the finest orators ever to rise in the said House.

Irene fits exactly into Sandy's comedy of New Town manners – and mamas. As a book review in *The Scotsman* commented; 'she first realised Bertie's love of the theatre by the way he reacted *positively* to the rapid changes of light on the set of the Contemporary Theatre of Krakow's production in the Edinburgh Festival, to which she took him at the age of four months...'

Bertie after many years as a seven year-old, was to have his eighth birthday, the description of his chaotic party being the chapter I read to the audience in the marquee.

The chapter – and indeed the book – closed, as is

Sandy's custom, with a poem by Angus Lordie, an art-dealer character in the novel who is developing, if not into Burns, then certainly into a considerable lyric voice in his own right.

But Krakow... now there's a memory. There was a morning, years ago at a medical academic meeting in Philadelphia, where I appeared to arrive, not from Edinburgh but from Krakow. Delivered to the US slightly late by the World's Favourite Airline, the first Session had already started when I legged it up to the Registration desk.

'Welcome to the States, Dr Purdie,' said the charming lady Registrar, handing me the satchel with the Programme, correction *Program*, list of delegates, social events etc. Seeing my hands were now full, her assistant, picked up my ID badge from the dozens lying in A-Z sequence on the registration desk. She then leaned forwards and kindly pinned it on to my jacket.

'Thank you, ladies,' said I and headed off for the lecture hall, thinking all was well with the world. It was not. She had pinned on the ID badge of the delegate right next to me in the alphabetical sequence.

I went into that first session of the Conference completely unaware that I was not:

Dr DW Purdie,
Edinburgh, UK

I was:

Dr DZ Purzhynski
Krakow, Poland

By sheer chance at that first session, I did not encounter any other UK delegate who would have instantly spotted the error; and of course you never look at your own ID. Why would you, it's you.

All went well until the mid-morning coffee break, at which I was approached by a large, beaming American delegate unknown to me. He shook my hand with patriotic vigour, saying,

'Welcome to the US, doctor.'

'Thank you. Always happy to be over here.'

'Great. D'you mind my asking if you're comfortable speaking conversational English?'

'Er…*yes*. I think my English is coming on quite well.'

'Great. Well, my granddaddy was born in Krakow.'

'Really? How incredibly interesting…'

'Yeah. Well, not right *in* Krakow, in Zwierzyniec. It's like, a few clicks to the West of it. He was in the boot business. I guess the boot trade is still a big deal in Krakow, right?'

'I'm sure it is; yes, absolutely.'

There then followed the most extraordinary conversation in which I was faced with a set of questions, all of which seemed to relate to the current political and cultural position of Poland. As a good European I did my best but could only answer these enquiries in the most superficial, inconsequential and clearly unsatisfactory manner – to the increasing restlessness of my American colleague, who eventually said,

'You've like just *arrived* from Europe?'

'Yes. Just off the plane.'

'Ok. So how are things in Krakow?'

'In *Krakow*? I haven't the faintest idea. But look, if you contact the Polish Consulate-General here in Philadelphia, I'm sure they'll be able to help you.'

'I gotta go. But let me just say...you speak *real* good English'.

'Thank you; and if I may say so, so do *you*!'

And thus, in mutual mystification, we parted.

I was then hailed by a passing delegate whose ID Badge ended, 'Poznan, Poland'.

'Witam! Mam właśnie przybył z Polski?'

What in God's name was going on? I said,

'Stop! Look, I *only* speak what passes for English in this country.'

'Excellenty! I too will only English speaking here. Is great practice for us, no?' He pointed at my ID badge.

'You just in from Krakow?' I looked down...

I still have Dr Perdinski's ID tag somewhere – and am not afraid to use it... I leave for Boston tomorrow to give a talk at The Country Club at Brookline, Boston, which is celebrating the centennial of Golf's coming of age in America.

How did this happen? All will be revealed.

Meanwhile, *Dobranoc i słodkie sny!*

Machrihanish

Office of the Dean

St Andrew's College
King George IV Bridge
Edinburgh EH1 1EE

THE COLLEGE owns an 'Outstation' in remote south Argyll, whence I have just returned with a group of colleagues after a strenuous weekend of walking, thinking, golfing and drinking – in short, we have been in nirvana. Here, jaded Dons and Deans can don faded jeans and spend a few days in peace and reflection. The location of this highland Shangri-La is Machrihanish, virtually at the tip of the Mull of Kintyre. Sometimes when a major policy rethink is required at College, or when a group of Dons request a break to complete a major paper or a grant application, I will say gravely,

'Right, I think we should Mull this over!' and next weekend it's off to Kintyre.

The centrepiece of our retreat is Dalmore House, a two-storey erection of uncertain age above the beach near Machrihanish village. It looks due west to the Hebridean islands of Islay and Jura, beyond which there's nothing till Nova Scotia. It was given to us a year or so back by a wealthy ex-Fellow of the College whose invention of the Bathing Wig™ has been such a boon to male baby-boomers, now thickening below and thinning above. Dalmore is also within sight of our on-shore marine biology research station and 'The Kraken', our off-shore tidal serpent. The latter is indeed a giant sea monster, but mechanical rather than biological, its prey being tidal surges. These it gobbles up and converts to electricity to be ingested by the National Grid. It's proving to be a powerful harvester of energy from the rip-tides which race past the southern end of Argyll between Scotland and Co. Antrim in Ireland, clearly visible just ten miles away. Although only half the breadth of the English Channel, no one has ever swum our North Channel and no one ever will, thanks to the sheer power of those tides. If our Dear Leader, Ms Sturgeon is right and the Pentland Firth is the 'Saudi Arabia of *wave* power', then the North Channel is the proof of Shakespeare's remarkable foresight on renewables in *Julius Caesar*:

'There is a tide in the affairs of men,
Which, taken at the flood, leads on to fortune'

Kintyre, from the Gaelic *ceann tir* (the head-end of the land) is a remarkable piece of real estate. It not only looks south to Antrim and Rathlin island where Robert Bruce saw the famous spider, but also east to Arran and the distant Ayrshire coast. Looking west, in addition to Islay, there is Gigha of the *Na h-Eileanan a-staigh*, 'the inner isle' of the Southern Hebrides.

The Gaelic language is extinct now among the locals here and that is a pity, since the splendidly named Dr Aonghais Mhor MacEachran, my Head of Celtic Studies, tells me it was a particularly pure form of the old Irish Q-Celtic. My own maternal grandfather, a farmer in Kintyre and born in 1863, had it beaten out of him at Campbeltown Grammar School, corporal punishment being liberally applied to any child caught speaking the tongue of his ancestors in preference to that of the *sassenach*, the Saxon.

He also remembered overhearing two shepherds talking on the day that Lord Lorne, son and heir of his landlord the Duke of Argyll, was being married to Princess Louise, daughter of the Queen. His Grace of Argyll, by the way, is the head of Clan Campbell and is still known in these parts by his Gaelic title of *MacChalein Mhor* or 'son of the great Colin' since his line descends from the patriarch Sir Colin Campbell of Loch Awe and Ardscotnish.

Anyway, there was no doubt in the shepherds' minds as to who was doing who the favour in these nuptials which, Aonghais advises me, took place at Windsor in 1871. With all the fierce clan-pride of the Highlander, one shepherd said to the other:

'Aye Dougal, it is the proud, *proud* wumman that Queen Victoria must be this day, to see a daughter o' hers and yon Cherman Albert being mairrit onto a son of *MacChalein Mhor...!*'

Aonghais himself, a man of Islay and a fluent Gaelic

speaker took our group from Dalmore down to Southend, the village closest to the actual *maol*, or headland, where Kintyre finally falls into the sea. Here we were shown the famous 'footsteps of Columba', two foot-like impressions in a rock on the hillside where, says local tradition, the Saint stood in 563AD on his first arrival in Scotland; and wept because he could yet see the hills of Antrim.

'Right, brethren, back to the *currach* and shove off!' the Saint must have cried to his long-suffering monks as they trooped back to their flimsy hide-covered boat.

'Shove *off*? Where to this time?' they must have asked.

'Iona. Now *row*!'

Back at Machrihanish we had an expedition to the Kintyre Seabird and Wildlife Observatory which is essentially a large hut lashed to a rocky promontory. From this the Warden, Eddie Maguire, maintains a record of the extraordinary range of wildlife that flies or swims into his ken. The sheer volume of fishing is remarkable. Squadrons of gannets from Ailsa Craig peel off and plunge in, cormorants and shags dive after them, sleek sea otters recline on offshore skerries between fishing trips, while fat Atlantic Grey seals roll about on sandbars on the outer beach. It's remarkable that there's a fish left in the sea.

Meanwhile, exotic species such as the Roseate Tern, the Grey Phalarope and even a Sabine's gull enliven the scene. Mention of the latter produced a splendid fire-fight after supper back at Dalmore between two of my biologists. When I finally retired they were still slugging it out as to whether the Sabine's gull was the *sole* species of the genus *Xema*, i.e. was it *Xema sabini* or was it just another species of the genus *Larus*, i.e. *Larus sabini*? This is apparently of seismic importance.

I left them to it.

Ah, the joys of academia Argyll-style. Retiring to the sound of the dull thud and long swish of Atlantic combers landing and rolling up the beach below, I subsided gently in the arms of Morpheus.

Sabine's Gull

Cormorant

Roseate Tern

Grey Phalarope

Bunny Rabbit

Sea Otters

The Dean on the Phone

Office of the Dean

St Andrew's College
King George IV Bridge
Edinburgh EH1 1EE

OUR COLLEGE telephonist, the formidable Miss Elsie Carruthers is under strict instruction *not* to forward any messages to me from 'Cold Callers'. I have become seriously irritated with these unsolicited offers of redundant intimacies or commercial ventures, some even offering extensions to my 'equipage', whatever that is. However, should any of them penetrate our outer defences, I have developed a useful means of clearing the line. Thus:

Caller: Hi Professor! How are you today?

Dean: *Much* better, thank you. The bleeding's *almost* stopped now; and y'know that er...*other* thing? Well, quite a lot of it came away last night...

Click.

A different and rather more intellectual response is adopted by Prof. Archibald Mackendrick, my Chair of Formalistic Logic and one of the brightest men in the country. We suspect he plugs himself into the mains overnight to recharge his necktop computer.

Cold Caller: Hi, Prof. Archie! How are you today?

AM: Why thank you. How *very* kind of you to enquire. However, it rather depends on what you mean by '*How*', doesn't it? – which is *itself* predicated on whether you're utilising '*You*' in its singular or plural identity, i.e. referring to *me*, or collectively to my Department in the sense of, *Le Départment, c'est moi!*; while all *that* is contingent on whether you're deploying '*Today*' as a referent to the *present* day, i.e. 4th February, or to the present *era*, in contrast to 'yesteryear' or 'futurity' within the Einsteinian space-time continuum.

Also, the logical sequence of your...

Click.

Then there is the auto-answerphone wheeze, dreamed up by Dr Fred Flaxman of our Telecoms Research Unit. All that's required is a child's beeper costing a few pence. Held to the phone, it's *beeped* at the end of your 'Recorded Message' – but it's actually you *in propria persona* on the line...

Thus: *Ring-ring, ring-ring...* (pick up)

Dean: You've reached the Dean's Office at St Andrew's College. Leave me a message at the tone. *Beep!*

Caller: Morning, Dean. Dr James Hutton here, Trinity College, Oxford. Sorry to miss you. I was wondering if you...

Dean: Your call is being recorded for unspecified purposes.

Hutton: I see. I was wondering if you could call me back...

Dean: Error! The name given was 'Hutton'. Why should you be called 'Back'?

Hutton (aside): This is a bloody odd message...

Dean: Expletive deleted! This phone is obscenity-sensitive.

Hutton: Holy Christ, it's *interactive*...

Dean: *And* blasphemy-aware. We will pray for you... *Click*.

The telephone is also a grand medium for the dying art of the practical joke. This is an institution now succumbing, like so many innocent pleasures, to PC and the dreaded Healthy & Safe Executive.

A friend of mine is the CEO of a major finance house in Edinburgh, that is when he's not on the high seas, racing or cruising in his beloved yacht the *Lady Rosalind*.

At the Forth Marina on the south bank of the river last autumn, I found him raging about the state of the warps. These are ropes securing the yacht to one of the marina's pontoons.

'Just *look* at these effing warps! They're chafing *hard* on the pontoon. Just *one* gale sending big swells into the marina and the thing could part. The *Rosalind*, plus pontoon, would drift right out into the effing *river!* I've told them *repeatedly* to fix it, but oh no, nothing doing. It's a total disgrace!'

A fortnight later, and the morning after a really big gale, his (innocent) PA put a phone call through to him – from me.

She told him that on the line was 'Commander Julian

Richards, RN', from HMS *Caledonia*, the Royal Navy's shore base at Rosyth, directly across the Forth. (Incidentally, the accent of Cdr Richards made Prince Charles sound like a welder...)

Richards: Mr Williams, are you the owner of a sloop-rigged yacht, the *Lady Rosalind*?

Williams: I am.

Richards: Was she secured on a pontoon at Forth Marina?

Williams: What? What d'you mean '*was*'?

Richards: Last night we had a Gale Force 8 gusting 9, from the NE. It seems that the swell setting into the marina caused her warps to part and she drifted out into...

Williams: *What?*

Richards: ...into the river. The wind and the ebbing tide then carried her across to our facility here at RN Rosyth.

Williams: *What!* Commander, I *knew* this would happen! I've been telling them and *telling* them to fix those warps. They won't spend a *penny!* Just wait till I get hold of... wait, thank you *so* much for calling. Give me an hour to round up my crew and we'll come...

Richards: I'm afraid there's another problem. As you may know, RN Rosyth is a NATO nuclear facility. As such, our seaward entrance is protected by a screen of seabed magnetic mines...

Williams: *Mines?* That's not on the charts!

Richards: Of course it's not on the charts, Williams, it's secret.

Williams: **What!** The Forth is *mined* – and it's *secret?*

Richards: Do please calm down, Williams. It's not as bad as you might think. We've got *most* of the wreckage here...

(Long pause...)

Williams: Is that you, David?

Click!

The Dean in America

The University Club of New York

1 W. 54th St.
New York City
NY, 10019
USA

I AM PRESENTLY ON Spring vacation from St Andrew's
College which I have left in the hands of the Senior
Tutor, the Bursar and my Secretary/PA, Mrs Grimhilde
von Reichenau-Strelitz. I am currently midway through a
most instructive 3-week lecture tour of our ex-colonies,
subjecting academic audiences from Boston, Mass.
to Baltimore, Maryland to harangues on the Scottish
Enlightenment. This afternoon, however, I am at last
to be evacuated to play some golf (and lecture on the
subject) at Winged Foot, a golf Club occupying an estate
slightly smaller than Denmark and just north of New
York City.

American interest in the history of our game is
intense, the locals being keen to know if the modern
game did originate with the Scots. Alternatively, was it a
variant of *Kolf* from the Netherlands, which was
apparently being played as early as 1690 at the Dutch
colony of Fort Oraanje on the Hudson River. This was

long before golf arrived in South Carolina from Scotland in the 1740s.

The Chinese have also been busily at work here, alleging that their game of *Chui Wan*, ('hit ball – with stick' in Mandarin), was the original game. Indeed to the consternation of the R&A, the Cultural Ministry in Beijing has now released a 15th century print of the Emperor Wu Ping playing a ball towards a hole with a flag in it. I patiently explained that Ch'ui Wan was clearly brought to China from Scotland, probably from North Berwick where, to this day, the tenth hole on that great links is named *Eastward Ho!* This commemorates the arrival, in 1430, of a Chinese squadron in the Firth of Forth and the sensational disruption of the Lothian Open by a landing party of armed marines escorting Admiral Zheng Ho.

Now, I am not making this up. Zheng Ho was a real admiral, commanding a fleet of large ocean-going junks. He returned to China with the game, his home port of Wusan being now hailed in the Orient as 'The Ho of Golf'.

Last week I received an invitation from friends in Maryland to attend a 'ball game' over in Washington DC. This proved to be a baseball match between the local team, the Washington Nationals and the San Francisco Giants. Having been a keen cricketer in my youth and never having seen live baseball, I was keen to attend. As is well known, baseball evolved from cricket, just as their 'football', with its armored players and outrageous forward passes, evolved from rugby.

Right enough, baseball proved to be as far from cricket as New York is from Kirriemuir. The whole thing is illegal. For example, in my view the pitcher (bowler) was guilty of the most blatant throwing from the very start. I watched as he subjected a series of hapless batters (batsmen) to an unending series of full tosses, wides, no-balls and flagrant beamers, all totally ignored by the Umpire. The batter swung furiously and usually fruitlessly at the occasional ball within reach, but the game largely consisted of the pitcher and the catcher (wicket-keeper) throwing the ball to each other, to the noisy delight of the 45,000 crowd. All quite astonishing.

In the rare event of a connection, the batter then legged it in the direction of First Base (mid-off) where, if the fielded ball arrived before he did, it was a run-out. Hitting the ball anywhere to the rear from square-leg round to cover-point was a 'foul' and it was thus no surprise that after two hours of this behavior – and *six* innings by each side – not one single run had been scored! There would have been 150 scored in any competent game of cricket, which is nevertheless dismissed outright by the colonists as 'boring', convinced as they are that the result is *always* a draw.

Even more disappointing for myself at this game was the non-appearance of the 'sausage mortar'. This is a device similar to the military variety, i.e. a near-vertical steel tube with a propellant gas canister at its bottom, which fires pre-cooked sausages into the crowd. Its absence was apparently due to problems at the previous game; when the sausage blasted out of the mortar barrel, the force of the slipstream had stripped off its protective wrapping and that of the accompanying sachets of ketchup and mustard. This resulted in fans in the bleachers (cheap seats) being regularly splattered with red and yellow condiment, while the naked sausage sailed on up to the appreciative nobs in the galleries. Anyway, the game which I saw finally ended, after *nine* innings each, in a 2–0 win for the Nationals to the delight of the crowd which streamed off to 'grab a dog', apparently a culinary treat; and probably the best way to actually get the runs...

But to return to golf; one remarkable feature of some older US golf clubs is an attitude to women which would attract lengthy prison sentences here, following the Equality Act (2010). At one venerable club in Columbus, Ohio, I was told that women were not only banned from the course and clubhouse, but might not even *leave the car* when delivering their husbands for a round. One evening, a wife who was dropping off her husband at the clubhouse for a Club Board meeting, asked for, and was sternly denied, the urgent use of a restroom (toilet). Giving her husband The Look, she swept off down the drive and when he got home she read the Riot Act.

'Do you know,' she snapped, 'that the nearest restroom to your goddam club is down at the very far end of the road, at the Bowery gas station? They threw me a rusty key with a piece of wood on the end of it. I was then sent round the back to find, and *use*, the dirtiest, most insanitary, spider-infested restroom in America. Something must be *done*!'

'Honey,' said her husband, 'I'm so sorry. You're absolutely right. Apologies. I'll raise it with the Board – and something *will* be done.'

A month later, as he got home from the next Board meeting, she was waiting;

'Well, was there action?'

'Honey, there was. They were just appalled at what happened to you. It will never happen again. The Board has voted $8,000 to upgrade the restroom at that gas station, to your *entire* satisfaction.'

The Dean in DC

Office of the Dean

St Andrew's College
King George IV Bridge
Edinburgh EH1 1EE

I AM NOW BACK IN harness after driving around the State of South Carolina on the wrong side of the road, prudently exhibiting their old Confederate flag which is based on our Scottish saltire. Visits to our ex-colonists in the New World are always invigorating; and it is new indeed. A 'Deli' across the street from my hotel in Charleston, South Carolina, proudly proclaimed:

Feeding the South – and a Century old (Est. 1998)

They are, however, fascinated with the old. Despite showing no sign of renewing allegiance to the Crown they are all a-twitter over the impending royal baby. Two years ago, America virtually stopped for The Wedding. Tens of thousands of ladies arranged parties; met in someone's front parlor; put on hats; opened champagne; turned on CBS or NBC (they all carried it – *without* ads!) – and entered Westminster Abbey. Now it's the name of the royal infant, which is generating rivers of newsprint. I was repeatedly told, without concrete evidence, that it was going to be a boy – and that the name-range was severely limited.

'Since Independence here, back in 1776,' intoned a chap curiously described as an 'anchor' on a satirical TV show,

'the Brits have only used four names for their Kings. They need more! So we've sent one further name over to Bucking-ham Pal-ace, tellin' their Royalties that a good ol' US handle will give the dynasty noo life and vigor (sic).

'We can now reveal the odds offered by the London bookies on the four old names – and ours. They go:

2:1 George
3:1 William
4:1 Edward
5:1 Charles
500,000 :1 *Elvis!*
Aw, c'mon guys – Elvis was King!'

My trip began in the Deep South, in Greenville South Carolina to be precise, where I harangued the citizenry in their excellent Upcountry Museum – on the role of the Scots in the War of Independence. Ben Franklin, visiting Edinburgh in 1771 – with his son, who was later to stay loyal to the Crown – persuaded his host, the philosopher David Hume, of the iniquity of taxation without representation in the Commons. Both Hume and his great chum Adam Smith advocated relaxation of the fiscal stranglehold we had on our 13 North American colonies, which ran at the time from New Hampshire to Georgia. All to no avail. The King wouldn't hear of it, telling his colonist to shut up and behave or it would be war. And war it was – a civil war at that.

I once saw a splendid sketch on the subject in a Festival Fringe show. Just off a ship from Boston, an exhausted messenger with the news from Concord, Mass., of 'the shot heard round the world' is propelled into the royal presence. Covered in dust and grime, he throws himself down before George III who is not amused at the interruption to his whist.

KG III: Well? *Out* with it!

Messenger (panting): Sire, it's… it's our American colonists!

KG: Not *again*! For God's sake man, what is it *this* time?

Messenger: Sire, they're… they're *revolting*!

KG: But we *know* that! Tell us what they're *up to*?

Still flying my Confederate banner, I drove from Greenville to Columbia SC to examine the Burns and Walter Scott papers at the University there. Before leaving, however, I had time to visit the Greenville Highland Games. Absolutely remarkable. There were men there wearing so much plaid (tartan), woad, armour, weaponry and headdresses that they exhibited considerable difficulty on rising to their feet. Down from the Blue Ridge Mountains to the Games come the folks of the old migration – the Ulster Scots. And today they're just as thrawn, obstroculous and proudly independent as their ancestors back in Co. Antrim and Down. The accents have changed, but the attitude – never!

The trip ended in Washington with a visit to the Hill and a morning audience with Rob Portman, one of the two Senators from Ohio. Suave and assured after 20 years on the Hill, Portman deftly summarised the central issues before the country. He reviewed his own actions on the current flow of Bills and then took questions from his guests. The whole, performance was impressive and illuminating.

The DC experience left me wondering about the F-word, the political one. The Americans have had, since their Civil War, 150 years of making a Federal system work. So have our cousins up in Canada and down in Australia and New Zealand. All these nations have varying degrees of independence; for the States in Australia and the Provinces in Canada, leaving defence and monetary policy to the Union.

We gave them birth – we also gave them the English language – *habeas corpus* – trial by jury and the separation of the Judiciary from the Executive. They followed our lead; should we, perhaps, now follow theirs? I think we'll have a debate on the F-word in the College. Let battle commence.

Golf in America

Office of the Dean

St Andrew's College
King George IV Bridge
Edinburgh EH1 1EE

THE END OF Whitsun term gives St Andrew's a welcome summer break from shoving and kicking at the frontiers of knowledge and also the chance to catch up with fellow kickers and shovers abroad.

I took the time whilst in South Carolina, to inspect the historical arrival of Scotland's greatest sporting export; the pastime known to our stern ancestors as *The Ancyent & Healthfulle Exercyse of the Golffe*. With the Open Championship looming down the road at Muirfield, I have just indulged my amateur interest in the history of Golf by being interviewed by NBC, the American TV channel. The subject was the discovery by a colleague, that golf first hit the beaches of the New World as early as 1739 at Charleston. The consignment of drivers mashies, niblicks and brassies (no numbering of clubs in those days) left Leith in a sailing ship and arrived three months later in the fourth largest city among our 13 colonies from New Hampshire to Georgia.

Leith Links, now a public park, is where it all began.

It was probably in the mid-14th century after the Treaty of Northampton brought peace with England, that it dawned on our ancestors that the great linksland along our coastline were ideal for a certain game. Our hardy forefathers, having noticed how far a rounded pebble could be hit with a discarded deer antler, set to work to conceive, bring to birth and then codify a sport now enjoyed by 50 million worldwide.

So there I was in the US, naturally wearing my new golfing 'Plus 2s' from Kinloch Andersons of Leith, an extremely snappy outfit. I was, however, unaware that the said Plus 2s are known as 'knickerbockers' in the colonies, shortened of course to knickers with mutual confusion.

'Hey, how long have y'all been wearin' knickers?'

'I *beg* your pardon, sir…'

Anyway, the sternest test of golf in America is the Fir Dale Golf Club in Pennsylvania, a course whose rough is so tall and dense that balls, clubs, caddies and sometimes smaller members fail to emerge from it. I gave a speech at their Centennial and moved on to the nearby Merion Club where the US Open had just been sensationally won by England's Justin Rose. Playing that golf course brought back a memory of my first tour with the University's Golf Team when I was a stripling young lecturer and when my own golf ball became the subject of enquiry.

It happened in this wise:

I and my partner Colin Dalgetty from St Andrews

were in trouble; we were three down after nine. Waiting to play my approach to the short par-4 tenth hole, one of our American opponents strolled over and said,

'Guys, I have a question about your ball.'

Now, I was then a member of the Golf Society of the Caledonian Club, the old Scottish club in London's Belgravia. We have our own ball which bears, in crimson and royal blue, the Caledonian's magnificent coat-of-arms, replete with shield, crest and Latin motto. All this heraldry is not painted on the ball. It is *stippled* just under the surface, a form of tattooing.

I was alarmed. Did my ball in some way contravene some local American rule? My opponent went on,

'Man, I have to ask. Is that your *own* family coat-of-arms on the ball?'

I thought to myself, 'three down after nine... and I *am* a member of the Caledonian...'

'Yes it is, actually.'

'Wow...'

Two hours later and back in the locker room, my opponent was overheard talking to the American Captain and was saying,

'*And*, he has his family's coat-of-arms tattooed on his *balls!*'

'No!'

'*Yeah!*'

'But... how do *you* know?'

Keeping up the theme, tomorrow the NBC team will come with me to the National Records of Scotland at

Register House to film the actual Act of Parliament of 1457 when an exasperated King James II enacted:

Thyt ye Game of ye Futeballe – and of ye Golffe
– be utterlye cryit doun and nocht usit.
[Condemned and abandoned]

For when our ancestors *should* have been busy practising at weekends with longbow, sword and battle-axe for the next international stroke play encounter with England, were they so engaged? No they were not. They were out on the links, practising their bunker recoveries and their driving, to the uncontrolled irritation of the King. His Majesty had to back down eventually because Scots of any century are not to be denied their sporting heritage

'No taxation without recreation!' I hear them cry.

I visualise them standing by the old bridge over the Swilcan Burn at St Andrews, woods and irons in hand, splendidly defiant. To paraphrase the great 'Concord Hymn' of Ralph Waldo Emerson:

By the rude Bridge that arched the flood
Their flag of St Andrew now unfurled
Here once the embattled Golfers stood
And hit the shots heard round the world...

What a legacy they left us. In the early evening of next Sunday the eyes of Caledonia will be on the golf links of Muirfield in East Lothian. There, after four days of tremendous competition, millions worldwide will watch a grown man lift, and then kiss, a jug.

College Burns Nicht

Office of the Dean

St Andrew's College
King George IV Bridge
Edinburgh EH1 1EE

THE COLLEGE'S Burns Supper, a highlight of our Candlemas term, was held last night in Great Hall, which seems to have survived the occasion without structural damage. This is more than can be said for my more boisterous colleagues who regard Burns Night as open season for all manner of misbehaviour, fuelled as usual by industrial quantities of *Uisge Beatha*.

'Suffering this morning, are we?' I enquired of a bleary-eyed Bursar, whose breath alone would have restarted the College generator.

'Afraid so, Dean; it's *third*-degree Burns again,' was the gruff response as he lumbered off to the coffee machine.

Our Burns night is one of the oldest in the country, dating back to 1802 when the poet's grave in Dumfries was rather less green than some of his devotees in the Common Room this morning.

I have to MC the proceedings, being a co-editor of the *Burns Encyclopaedia*, and began by explaining to our

curious overseas Fellows and Dons what was likely to happen. The menu itself needed interpretation for the uninitiated, trumpeting 'Ongauns' on one side with the Recitations and Songs and 'Ingauns' on the other side with the bill of fare.

'Can you all hear me at the back?' I began innocently, only to see our resident wag, philologist Archie McIntyre, rise and say,

'Yes Dean, indeed I can; but very happy to swap with someone who *can't*.' Ribald laughter greeted this insolence. The 'Selkirk Grace' then followed, whereupon the Bursar, charged with the 'Address to the Haggis', announced its impending arrival in Hall.

'In five minutes, Messrs MacKenzie and Stuart of the Dept. of Music, will pipe in the Haggis – and in five hours it'll be piped out again, by Messrs Armitage Shanks of Barrhead!'

(For the uninitiated, this firm is a manufacturer of toilet porcelain).

The evening then followed its predictable pattern of songs, recitation and speeches, the highlight of which was the Reply to the 'Toast to the Lassies' by Professor Dorothy Finlander of Harvard University. Dotty is with us for a year to research the role of women in British public life. She is learning to shed the wondrous prolixity of US academia in her contacts with our rather more laconic citizens. Said she to Dr Charles Robertson a sociologist of unusual brevity,

'Dr Robertson, among your Scottish women is there

much discussion on psycho-social postnatal cybernetic feedback problem situations?' Charlie thought for a moment,

'Madam, in the tenements of Edinburgh, they speak of little else...'

Dotty's speech put Man – or rather *men* – firmly in their place. She pointed out that Burns himself had given women pride of place in the scheme of things when he wrote:

> All Nature swears, the lovely Dears,
> Her *noblest* work she classes, O,
> Her *'prentice* hand she tried on Man,
> And *then* she made the Lasses, O!'

Women, we were told, are much tougher than men, living on average of seven years longer than their male partners – mainly due to avoidance of excessive carnivorous eating, drinking of mind-altering fluids and inhalation of rolled-up burning plants.

Above all, there is their great feat. In just 270 days, a woman produces, from a single cell ten times smaller than a pinhead, the most complex object in the known Universe. Nothing detected by the Hubble Space telescope, we were assured, comes even *close* to the intricacy of a newborn infant. This assemblage is composed of 20 trillion cells organised into 16 integrated organ systems, surmounted by a supercomputer with a 600 GB random-access memory.

'Further consider, gentlemen,' she thundered, 'that a

woman does this almost always without error and moreover delivers it on time, on budget, and *alive*. Beside this colossal achievement the *male* contribution to the process is seen for what it is – a pale, limp and pathetic… thing!'

She's right of course.

'What would men be without women?' Mark Twain was asked.

'Scarce, Sir, *mighty* scarce', was the sage's sage reply.

The Burns Night ended, or rather was meant to end, with a Toast to The Immortal Memory of Burns by my old friend Prof. Willy Cruikshank of Glasgow, the greatest living authority on the Bard. However, when he got up to speak it was already ten minutes past midnight; the game was clearly up. He said,

'Dean, Dons and Fellows of St Andrew's College; Good *Morning!* I had not realised when I accepted your kind invitation, that his was *two-day* Dinner… so may I wish you all a very good night!'

And down he sat to thunderous applause – headed by me – after a speech which had lasted all of 30 seconds.

It was time, high time, for 'Auld Lang Syne'.

The Dean's Ivanhoe

Office of the Dean

St Andrew's College
King George IV Bridge
Edinburgh EH1 1EE

THE COLLEGE HAS now regained its summertime academic serenity with the thankful departure of the Edinburgh Festival Fringe. We have had three shows in our main lecture theatre over the past month, one of them labelled 'New Comedy' if a parade of scatological and gynaecological observations delivered at 160 decibels by an unshaven person may be so defined.

Otherwise it's been a relatively peaceful week with only the arrest in Shanghai of Prof. Gilbert Osram to enliven things. The distinguished head of our Institute of Sinology had been attending a seminar on ancient Chinese poetry. In a lecture on Wu Hs'ien Li, apparently a writer of the Pong Dynasty, Gilbert chose to describe his work as 'obscure'. Anyway, that is what he *meant* to say, but a tiny error in his pronunciation of the correct Mandarin word *móhu* led to it coming out as 'reeking of the dung of a he-goat'. This led to an impressive riot, the police were called and Osram found himself in a People's Court charged with an impressive range of public order offences. Unfortunately, he chose to defend himself in Mandarin when, stop me, did he not describe the People's Judge's opening statement as 'obscure' using the same mispronunciation that had landed him there in the first place! The judge blew a gasket and Osram found himself in a Chinese pokey for six weeks without the option.

That's the trouble with such a group of noisy, outspoken and combative academics as we have here; those very qualities that win them glittering prizes tend to give great offence to *apparachniki* in less enlightened realms. And now to cap it all, I hear that Orlando de Figueres, my Head of Hispanic Studies, has been caught starkers in a Manila flophouse with *four* local lovelies and a *hookah* containing an 'unknown' substance. Bet I know what it is...

Right; on a completely different tack, I have now completed a labour of love – and of 18 months. This is an abridgement, or redaction, or condensation, call it what you will of Sir Walter Scott's classic *Ivanhoe*. Come to think of it, the classical Greek term of ἐπιτομή (our *epitome*) is nearer the mark. As its etymology suggests, an epitome cuts away extraneous matter, leaving the kernel or marrow of the work intact and open to inspection. Scott, the 'Wizard of the North', is remembered with personal affection and admired as the inventor of the historical novel, but is little read nowadays. His collected works filled the bookshelves of our grandparents, the attics of our parents and the landfill sites of today – and that is a pity, for he was a brilliant storyteller. The general opinion has grown up that Scott, as novelist, is both long and 'difficult'. This probably arises from his writing when the printed word was the central means of communication, when attention spans were longer, distractions fewer and the historical novel a brilliant innovation.

Scott is still studied in college and university courses both in the UK and in continental Europe where his contribution to Romantic literature is secure. However, the non-academic reader now finds him prolix in dialogue, rambling in description and meandering in plot. The problem is actually the hardback covers of Sir Walter's books; they're simply far too far apart.

What I have done with the new edition is to preserve the storyline of *Ivanhoe* as well as the sights, sounds and smells of the Middle Ages which he evokes so well.

Social conflicts are always central to the plotlines within Scott and there's no shortage of them here. We have collisions between: Norman and Saxon; Monarch and Pretender; Cleric and Layman; Freeman and Outlaw; Jew and Gentile.

Scott's *dramatis personae*, such as Wamba the jester and Robin the Hood, are supplied with a drily ironic sense of humour as noble Saxons and despicable Normans fight it out with sharp words and sharper weapons. The great jousting tournament at Ashby de la Zouche resounds to thunderous crashes as Ivanhoe's lance dumps Norman after Norman on his armoured backside. This he does using weaponry supplied, or more accurately *leased* to him on a sale-or-return basis by the canny Hebrew, Isaac of York. We also have Scott's finest female portrayal in Isaac's daughter Rebecca, a Jewish intellectual and consultant physician. Rebecca rises to stratospheric heights of moral rectitude while her would-be seducer, the Templar Sir Brian de Bois Guilbert sinks to fathomless depths of dastardliness. Neither Rebecca nor Rowena the Saxon heroine and future Mrs Ivanhoe, fall for the lecherous advances of their Norman pursuers, principally because both (pursuers, that is) are encased *cap a pié* in plate mail. Ladies, then as now, prefer their suitors to be suited by Brooks Bros rather than the blacksmith.

Robin Hood and Friar Tuck also show up, as does Richard *Coeur de Lion*, sprung from durance vile in Austria just in time to sort out the reptilian Prince John and his satraps. It's a terrific yarn.

The abridged or *epitomized* text runs to some 96,000 words, about the average for a modern novel, whereas the original had around 194,000.

'Spring *must* be coming,' opined a local newspaper when the story emerged in April, 'the knights are getting shorter!'

I am braced for stern criticism of the very concept of such an abridgement. Whatever the motive, no-one adjusts the text, or the musical score, or the brushwork, of a master and escapes scathless as Scott himself would say. However, if the present work leads modern readers back to the original masterpiece and indeed back to the greatest novelist himself, it will have served its purpose.

And it's still a thundering good read. It ends with the famous scene where Mrs Ivanhoe is closeted with her maidservant Elgitha on the morning after the wedding. There is no truth whatsoever in the rumour that Elgitha says, in Anglo-Saxon of course,

'*Hálettung, hlæfdige, ænig forþgang?*' (Well my Lady, how did it go?) Rowena sighs,

'*Ah! Swéte Ivåenhöe, beornwiga eftgemyndgan...*'

(Ah, dear Ivanhoe; a knight to remember...)

She then says, confidentially,

'*Lóclóca, hwonne átrendlaþ innan brýdbedd, Ooh – swelc ceald heaðureáf...*' (Only thing is, when he rolls over in bed; Oooh, all that cold armour...)

The Lady Mondegreen

Office of the Dean

St Andrew's College
King George IV Bridge
Edinburgh EH1 1EE

A GUEST LECTURE at St Andrew's College this week was given by the distinguished mediaevalist Dr Spencer Moran of Oxford. I greeted him warmly in the Deanery but also with profound apologies for the spelling errors in the flyer for his talk. Yesterday morning, the computer keyboards in our Secretariat decided, for some unfathomable reason, to replace every 'a' with an 'o'. Whether this was just a glitch, or sabotage, has yet to be determined. Whatever, it led to the startling announcement on College e-boards – and on our website – that a lecture, curiously entitled *The Bottle of Hostings*, would be delivered by 'Dr S Moron' of Oxford, chaired by 'the Deon'.

This seems to be a case of life imitating art, since I clearly recall something similar in a sketch by *The Two Ronnies*.

Ronnie Barker, as a 1960s BBC newsreader, began a bulletin by apologising for an autocue malfunction whereby every 'e' in capitalised words, had become an 'o'.

'Horo is the Nows' he intoned. 'The Primo Ministor, Sir Aloc Douglas-Homo…'

Anyway Spencer took it all in good part, not least because as a Fellow of New College Oxford he is a successor to that verbal gymnast Dr WA Spooner.

A painting of that delightful theologian and former Warden of the college, hangs above their High Table. Years ago, giving a speech there to a gang of Advocates and QCs, my eye was irresistibly drawn to the image of Spooner and my tongue into incipient spoonerisms. Mind you, many of those attributed to the old boy are apocryphal, but there are some well-attested gems: in Chapel one Sunday morning the congregation heard him intone:

'Let us now sing to God's praise, hymn number two hundred and fifty nine, 'Kinquering Kongs their Titles take…' while once in a sermon he assured his flock,

'Yes, my friends, the Lord is *indeed* a shoving leopard.'

Spooner has his imitators right here. Henry MacPherson our long-serving Head of Rhetoric & Belles-Lettres is a mischievous spoonerist.

'Is the Bean dizzy?' I overheard him enquire of my secretary in the outer office recently,

'Miss Harrison,' I called through from the Sanctum, 'tell him the Bean's extremely dizzy – and that he's a shining wit!'

Accuracy in the printed word is of course essential:

We should not write so that it is possible for the

reader to understand us, but so that it is impossible for him to misunderstand.

Thus wrote Marcus Fabius Quintilianus, the great Quintilian, funded by the Emperor Vespasian to teach rhetoric to the youth of Rome. His enlightened reign in the 1st century AD provided the philosopher David Hume's great *Treatise of Human Nature* with an epigraph from Tacitus:

Rara temporum felicitas ubi sentire quæ velis,
et quae sentias, dicere licet.
(Happy the times when one may think what one likes – and say what one thinks...)

Saying what one thinks is contingent on the times, as is writing what one likes. Here, even single-letter spelling errors can be embarrassing. As the witty chairman of a major Dundee publishing house once revealed in my hearing at a dinner, even a well-edited organ of record such as the *Courier*, can err... In such cases, we were told, it is essential that the apology and correction is carried by the next edition of the paper; and it is absolutely essential that the correction contains no spelling errors. Thus the *Courier*, reporting the arrest of some malefactor in central Dundee, advised that his detention was effected by a particular defective constable of the Dundee police force... next day, a contrite *Courier* made an unreserved apology to the detective constable concerned. This officer, readers were assured, was a long-serving and highly regarded member of the Dundee police farce.

Talking of verbal or literary misapprehensions, there is of course the Mondegreen. Coined by author Sylvia Wright in 1954, it originated in her misinterpretation of a line in that fine old Scots ballad *The Bonny Earl o' Moray*. Hearing, but not seeing, the verse:

Ye Highlands and ye Lowlands,
  Oh where hae ye been?
They hae slaine the Earl O' Moray
  And *layd him on the Green...*

Who, wondered Wright, was this mysterious and hitherto unknown 'Lady Mondegreen' who died with Moray – and, moreover, what had they been up to?

Our ballads seem to be prone to Mondegreenian errors of perception, particularly south of Hadrian's Wall. That great Jacobite lament, *Woe's me for Prince Charlie* was, deliberately, interpreted in England as 'Where's me fourpence, Charlie?' i.e. an aggrieved Scottish demand for payment, always a source of hilarity to our southern neighbours. Indeed as PG Wodehouse correctly pointed out in *Blandings Castle*, 'It is never difficult to distinguish between a Scotsman with a grievance – and a ray of sunshine...'

In modern times, the Mondegreen lives on: a line in The Beatles' 'Lucy in the Sky with Diamonds' was heard being sung in a Glasgow Karaoke bar as 'The girl with *colitis* goes by...'

Sometimes the Mondegreen is deliberate. Disgraceful hints of improper sheep-affection in the Hebrides have included the allegation that even the titles of popular songs have been altered to accommodate such alleged proclivities. For example, the title of The Rolling Stones' smash hit, 'Hey, You! Get offa my Cloud' has allegedly been changed to: 'Hey, McLeod! Get offa my Ewe!'

Needless to say, the Dons and Fellows of St Andrews College are meticulous essayists and orators whose devotion to the accuracy of the printed or spoken word is truly absolute.

The Dean in Musselburgh

Office of the Dean

St Andrew's College
King George IV Bridge
Edinburgh EH1 1EE

THE NEWS THAT Nicola Sturgeon has no intention of staging another Referendum on independence, the so-called 'Indyref', anytime soon, has triggered memories of the run-up to the last one. In September 2014, the College was shaping up for the Martinmas Term with the Dons straggling back from vacation after their usual disruption of various summer conferences, seminars and academic workshops.

I heard that Fergus Fergusson our rumbustious Head of Politics has been compiling a 'poll of polls' on voting intentions in the Referendum, his own view coming to light on BBC Two's *Newsnight* when he was asked bluntly which side he was on. Not wanting to appear biased or to be disbarred from lucrative TV appearances he clearly had to be non-committal. His cryptic reply was that he was 'a fan of Horace Walpole's home at Twickenham...'

What on earth could this mean?

I raised it at High Table over dinner the next day and there was much head scratching.

'It *must* be a cryptic clue,' I said. More head shaking, rumination and claret swirling followed, until our Professor of Music suddenly said,

'Got it! He's on about Strawberry Hill, that gothic castle of Horace Walpole's at Twickenham. There was an English pop band, The Strawberry Hill Boys – later shortened to The Strawbs – who had a smash hit in the '70s with a song called 'Part of the Union'.

I'd never heard the song before, but next day in the Deanery I had my secretary Harriet the Harridan play it to me on that extraordinary *YouTube* website. It proved to have such a catchy tune that I sent it to Alistair Darling, suggesting it as a rallying cry for his 'No' campaign.

✿ ✿ ✿

Last Thursday I went next door to the National Library of Scotland (NLS), our dear neighbours here on George IV Bridge. I was there to give a Talk on our recently completed *Burns Encyclopaedia*. The *Encyclopaedia* has been a major task, now thankfully completed: 810 Entries and 275,000 words to describe the Life & Times of the extraordinary farmer turned 'gauger' (Inland Revenue Executive) ranked a lyric genius by Keats and Wordsworth no less, and a master songsmith by Haydn and Beethoven.

The irony of the Burns story is that despite over 2,000 volumes dealing with his life and work, there remain intractable impressions, most but not all abroad, that he lived in penury and died of drink. The *Encyclopaedia* will correct any such impression for those enlightened souls fortunate enough to acquire a copy.

The Boardroom of the NLS makes a first-class lecture theatre with good acoustics and a big screen. The latter is vital as all my harangues are now delivered with images drawn from the national archive of images. These are held by Historic Environment Scotland and comprise nigh on half a million drawings, paintings, photographs, maps, audio and video clips all telling the nation's story over the fifteen hundred years of our history. All these treasures are available to teachers and scholars, and to the general public for a modest subscription fee.

For example, I recently went hunting for images of the original Musselburgh golf course to show to some visiting American historians studying the origins of the game in Scotland. Here the very first lady golfer, Mary Stuart, Queen of Scots, played the great game over 500 years ago; and on the same turf in use today. Quite remarkable.

✿ ✿ ✿

Mention of Musselburgh brings back the happy memory of speaking at the Musselburgh (Old) Golf Club dinner some years ago. This was just after I had taken possession of Duncan's Land, my Edinburgh apartment, which is 400 years old, with plumbing to match. I had also been trying to find a skilled joiner to fix up the bookshelves in the study.

The membership of Musselburgh 'Old' contains the tradesmen and worthies of the town, the salt of the good earth of East Lothian. The Club is actually a century older than my house. After the dinner, the Captain of this most hospitable club took me aside as I was getting ready to leave.

'Right Prof, yer lad's ootside, and we've pounded him.'

This turned out to mean that my taxi driver was at the door – and had been paid.

'And ye're no wanting nae payment?'

'No, Captain. Happy to be your guest at this famous links; a great pleasure, thank you.'

'There's naething ye're needin' then?'

Without thinking I said,

'Captain, what I actually need most at the moment is a joiner!'

'A *jyner*? Plenty here. Lads, the Prof needs a jyner!'

Ten days later my shelves were up – and paid for.

They're up yet...

The Dean's Correspondence

Office of the Dean

St Andrew's College
King George IV Bridge
Edinburgh EH1 1EE

THIS COLLEGE must be home to almost every registered eccentric in the academic world. The sheer range of issues and obsessions which exercise the Dons and Fellows is matched only by the sheer number of items they feel compelled to pile up in my in-tray and to jam in my inbox. No remonstrance stays the flow; no appeal stems the flood. Even threats that items of correspondence may be exhibited in The Dean's Diaries seem to be no deterrence.

Some recent exchanges appear below:

To: The Dean;
From: Dr JGL Mallard PhD FRS

I was outraged to receive your letter on Tuesday, presumably sent at the instigation of the Supreme Soviet which runs this place, regarding my 'personal freshness'. What the devil has it to do with you?

For the record, I had put in 16 straight hours on a hot steamy day in the Anti-Gravity Lab, which still has no AC. I slumped down in the Common Room for a Jeeves. Nobody complained, no clothes pegs were attached to noses. So, own up. Who's behind this?

Furthermore, you say that 'not infrequently' I leave an 'odoriferous sensation' behind me. This is outrageous. I come here to do *Science* – not to be sniffed and smelt. I am a Physicist, not a bloody Geranium!

Mallard

INTERNAL MEMO:

To: Chief Steward;
From: The Dean

Mr Perkins; what, pray, is this 'Jeeves' of Dr Mallard?

From: Chief Steward:

It's the 'restorative' drink served by Jeeves during his interview for the position of Gentleman's gentleman to Mr Bertie Wooster, as advertised in *The Times*. Observing that Mr Wooster was suffering from a monumental hangover (after a Dinner at the Drones Club), Jeeves prepared and then served his 'restorative' to Mr Wooster – with immediate effects. You'll find it in *Carry on, Jeeves* by P.G. Wodehouse, sir.

From Dean:

Really? What on earth was in it?

From Chief Steward:

It consists of a half pint of fresh tomato juice, to which are added, in strict sequence: Angostura Bitters; a raw Egg; Tabasco sauce; and a *modicum*, i.e. a major slug, of Oloroso sherry.

From Dean:

And what were these 'effects' on Wooster?

From Chief Steward:

Remarkably, the sun immediately rose. Birds settled on the windowsill and sang a merry roundelay; and Mr Wooster's tongue ceased to taste like a tram-driver's glove.

From Dean:

Have one sent up to the Deanery!

✿ ✿ ✿

By email from: The Very Rev. HJT Ponsonby HJTP@CofE.co.uk Dept. of Theology & Homiletics.

My Dear Dean,

Something really *must* be done about the main speech at Founder's Dinner. One attends this function hopefully to hear a serious disquisition on the College's history and Ordinances.

Our guest speaker last week, Dr 'Ollie' Offenbach from Cambridge was billed as a theoretical epistemologist, but turned out to be a rank humourist. He also required a haircut and was clearly wearing a *made-up* bow tie! His anecdotes and mimicry may have convulsed our madcap younger Dons, but could only be appreciated by persons who like *laughing*. It has to stop. Pray see to it.

Yrs sincerely,
Henry Ponsonby.

✿ ✿ ✿

To The Dean, St Andrew's College, Edinburgh
Dear Sir,

I am writing a history of the Scottish universities

and wondered if you could produce any *facsimile* of your Royal Charter, mentioned in your *Quatercentenary History* of 1961. I can't seem to find it online; the Lord Lyon says he doesn't have it and the Public Record Office deny its existence. You are truly medieval are you not? Haven't been having us on for centuries now, have you?

Yrs truly,
Prof. Herbert Quadriga.
University of Western Carolina

Dear Prof. Quadriga,

How dare you suggest that we are not, in any sense, middle-aged. We were founded in 1561 and received the Royal nod from King James VI & I in 1610 after the Union of the Crowns. His son King Charles I was a Hon. Fellow here, but was unfortunately beheaded before he could sign the Charter.

We petitioned Charles II to restart the process in 1660 after his Restoration, but he left the Charter document in the water-closet of Miss Nell Gwynne who used it to deal with, shall one say, a personal emergency. It hasn't been seen since.

However, you may rest assured that His Majesty told our then Dean, Sir Angus Carmyllie Bt., that he had most definitely signed it, he thought.

I trust this clarifies matters.

Yrs etc.
The Dean

✿ ✿ ✿

From: Dr Reginald Farrer;
Dept. of Semiotics

Dean, my Floribunda (*Stephanotis floribunda*) has produced a deep black mottling on its leaves for the second year now, despite treatment with pentaoxygenated xanthone.

I'm in despair. What do you suggest?

RH Farrer

From: The Dean

I suggest you *stop* writing to me with these ridiculous questions! I repeat for the nth time that I know absolutely *nothing* about Floribundas, or Clematis, or anything else that grows, or refuses to grow, in your domestic plot.

So why don't you rip out your Floribunda, drag it to Broadcasting House, and hurl it to the ground, mottled leaves and all, at *Gardeners Question Time*. Goodbye.

Some other books published by **LUATH** PRESS

Heart of Midlothian

Sir Walter Scott
Newly adapted for the modern reader
by David Purdie
ISBN: 978-1-908373-80-9 PBK £9.99

If a sister asks a sister's life on her bended knees, they will pardon her; and they will win a thousand hearts by it.

Edinburgh, 1736: Captain John Porteous is charged with murder and locked up in Edinburgh's Tolbooth prison, also known as the Heart of Midlothian. When news comes that he has been pardoned, a baying mob breaks into the jail, liberating its inmates and bringing Porteous to their own form of justice.

But one prisoner, Effie Deans, chooses not to take the opportunity to flee. Wrongly convicted of murder, Effie has been sentenced to death. Jeanie, her older sister, sets about walking to London to beg for her pardon from the queen.

A gripping tale of religious piety and filial devotion, this new edition of *The Heart of Midlothian* has been expertly reworked for modern readers by David Purdie.

Ivanhoe

Sir Walter Scott
Newly adapted for the modern reader
by David Purdie
ISBN 978-1-908373-58-8 HBK £19.99

Fight on, brave knights. Man dies, but glory lives!

Ivanhoe has been cut down to size in this modern retelling of Scott's classic novel: the original text has been slashed from an epic 194,000 words to a more manageable 95,000.

Banished from his father's court, Wilfred of Ivanhoe returns from Richard the Lionheart's Crusades to claim love, justice and glory. Tyrannical Norman knights, indolent Saxon nobles and the usurper Prince John stand in his way. A saga of tournaments and melees, chivalry and love, nobility and merry men, Ivanhoe's own quest soon becomes a battle for the English throne itself...

This is exactly what's needed in order to rescue Sir Walter Scott.
ALEXANDER McCALL SMITH

Knights getting shorter... [Ivanhoe] has been brought up to date by Professor David Purdie who is president of the Sir Walter Scott Society and should know the ropes.
HERALD SCOTLAND

Details of these and other books published by Luath Press can be found at: **www.luath.co.uk**

Luath Press Limited
committed to publishing well written books worth reading

LUATH PRESS takes its name from Robert Burns, whose little collie Luath (*Gael.*, swift or nimble) tripped up Jean Armour at a wedding and gave him the chance to speak to the woman who was to be his wife and the abiding love of his life. Burns called one of 'The Twa Dogs' Luath after Cuchullin's hunting dog in Ossian's *Fingal*. Luath Press was established in 1981 in the heart of Burns country, and now resides a few steps up the road from Burns' first lodgings on Edinburgh's Royal Mile.

Luath offers you distinctive writing with a hint of unexpected pleasures.

Most bookshops in the UK, the US, Canada, Australia, New Zealand and parts of Europe either carry our books in stock or can order them for you. To order direct from us, please send a £sterling cheque, postal order, international money order or your credit card details (number, address of cardholder and expiry date) to us at the address below. Please add post and packing as follows: UK – £1.00 per delivery address; overseas surface mail – £2.50 per delivery address; overseas airmail – £3.50 for the first book to each delivery address, plus £1.00 for each additional book by airmail to the same address. If your order is a gift, we will happily enclose your card or message at no extra charge.

Luath Press Limited
543/2 Castlehill
The Royal Mile
Edinburgh EH1 2ND
Scotland
Telephone: 0131 225 4326 (24 hours)
email: sales@luath.co.uk
Website: www.luath.co.uk